I just want to be... ME!

BUILDING RESILIENCE IN YOUNG PEOPLE

By Timothy Bowden Postgrad Dip Psych **and Sandra Bowden** M Ed (Couns Psych)

Illustrations by Sandra Bowden ~ Foreword by Dr Russ Harris

EXISLE
PUBLISHING

First published 2010

Exisle Publishing Limited
'Moonrising', Narone Creek Road, Wollombi, NSW 2325, Australia
P.O. Box 60–490, Titirangi, Auckland 0642, New Zealand
www.exislepublishing.com

National Library of Australia Cataloguing-in-Publication Data:

Bowden, Tim.

I just want to be me! / Timothy Bowden, Sandra Bowden

ISBN 9781921497476 (pbk.)

For children aged between 10 and 14.

Self-esteem in children.
Self-esteem in adolescence.
Self-perception in children.
Self-perception in adolescence.

Bowden, Sandra.

158.1

Designed by Alan Nixon
Typeset in Tarzana Narrow 14/15
Printed in Shenzhen, China, by Ink Asia

This book uses paper sourced under ISO 14001 guidelines from well-managed forests and other controlled sources.

10 9 8 7 6 5 4

Dedication

To our families and friends, who constantly remind us of what is important in life.

And Holly, our cat, who embodies the spirit of ACT (though she follows her stomach more than her heart).

Tim & Sandra Bowden

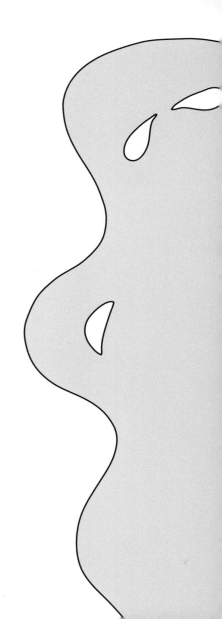

Foreword

Life is hard. And all human beings, young and old alike, will at times struggle with it. Everybody, no matter how talented, wealthy, famous, beautiful or successful they are, will at times fail, get rejected, make silly mistakes, screw things up, and get hurt both physically and emotionally. Everybody on the planet will at times feel sad, angry, anxious, lonely, fearful, guilty or lost. And we will all at times get entangled in painful negative thoughts: comparing ourselves unfavourably to others; judging ourselves harshly; dredging up painful memories from the past; rehashing old resentments and grievances; or worrying uselessly about the future.

Acceptance and Commitment Therapy, or ACT (which is said as the word 'ACT', not as the initials A-C-T), provides us with a scientifically proven framework for dealing more effectively with the inevitable pain of life. ACT teaches us how to connect with our values and live fully in the present moment; how to make room for painful feelings without being controlled or overwhelmed by them; and how to reduce the impact and influence of negative thoughts.

Learning happens best when students are entertained and stimulated by the content. Tim and Sandra Bowden obviously know this, and they have done a fantastic job in making ACT instantly accessible to children, parents and teachers through the creative use of words and pictures. When psychologist Steve Hayes created ACT in the early 1980s, he used a story to illustrate some of his ideas, about a bunch of scary-looking passengers on the back of a bus. In my own book about ACT, *The Happiness Trap*, I changed the story a bit: the passengers became demons and the bus became a boat. Tim and Sandra have now created their own version of this story in *I Just Want To Be ... ME!* — a comic book that not only entertains, but also instructs.

I Just Want to Be ... ME! shows us all how we can overcome our own psychological barriers and live richer, fuller lives. Everyone who reads it, from age five to age ninety-five, can learn much that is profound and useful. Indeed, I hope one day it becomes required reading in all schools; how much healthier our society would be if we could all learn these lessons early in life.

Dr Russ Harris
Bestselling author of *The Happiness Trap*

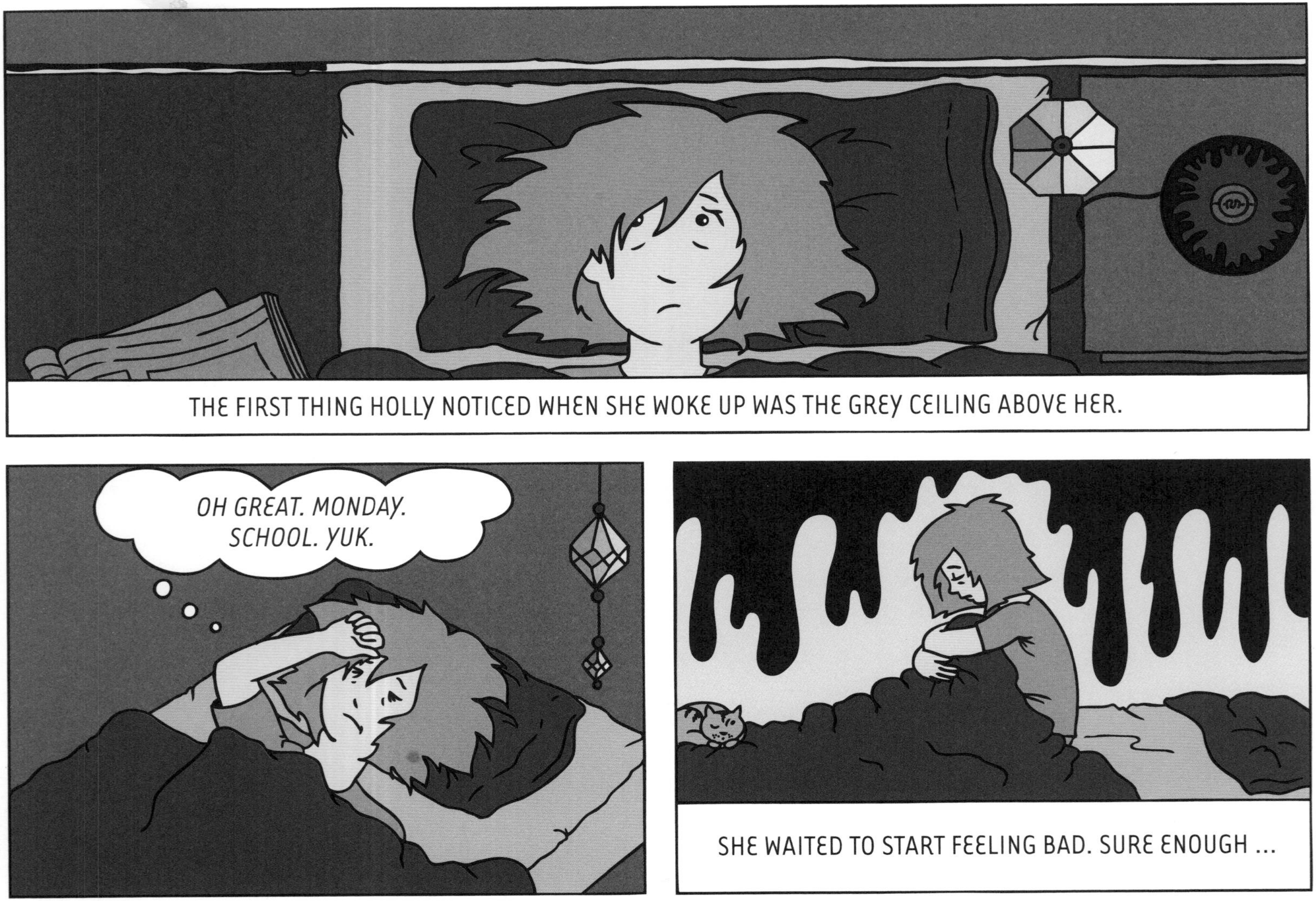
THE FIRST THING HOLLY NOTICED WHEN SHE WOKE UP WAS THE GREY CEILING ABOVE HER.
OH GREAT. MONDAY. SCHOOL. YUK.
SHE WAITED TO START FEELING BAD. SURE ENOUGH ...

SICK IN THE STOMACH ...

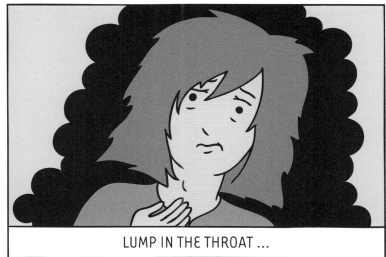

LUMP IN THE THROAT ...

TIGHT CHEST ...

BODY TOO HEAVY TO GET OUT OF BED ...

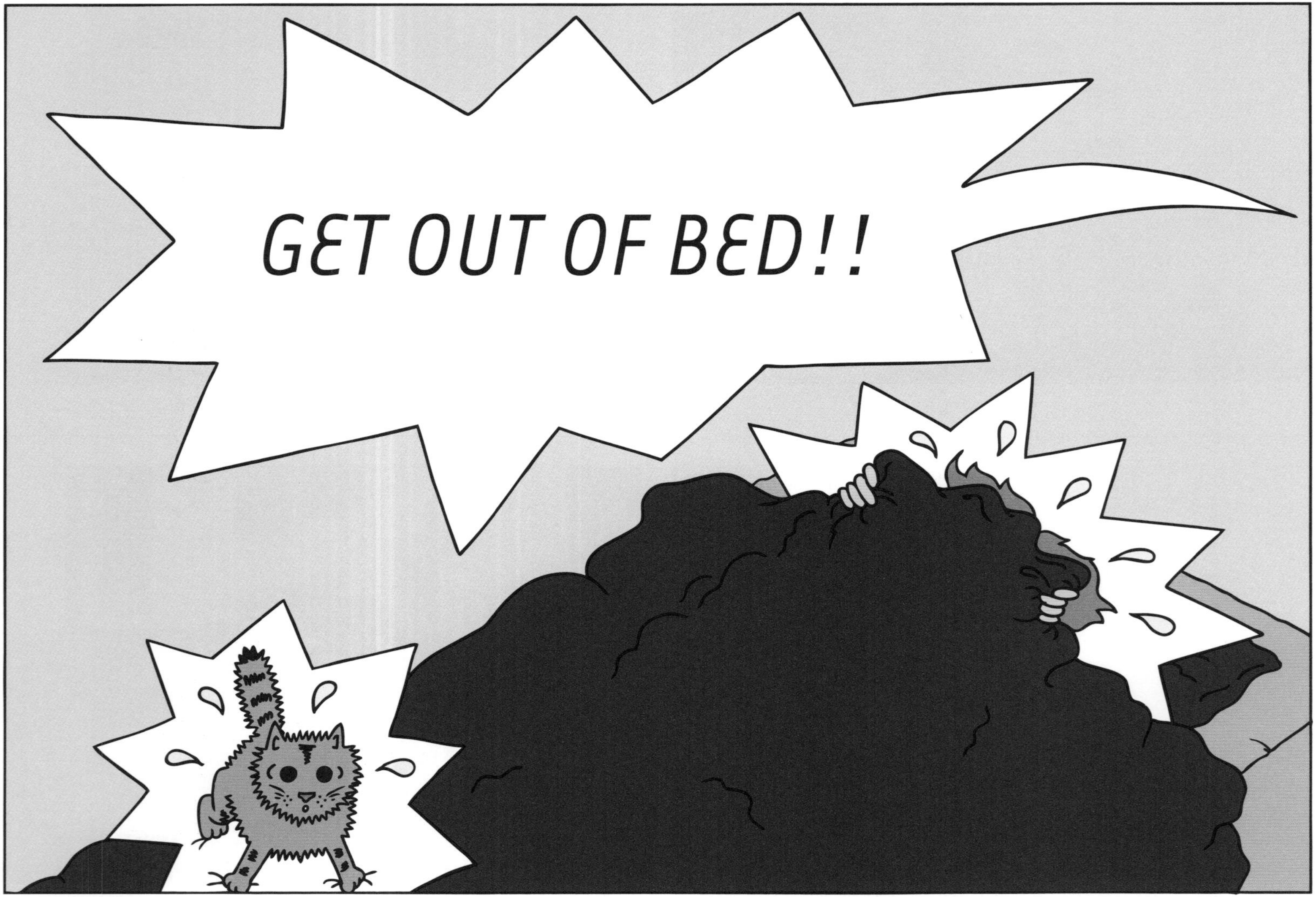
GET OUT OF BED!!

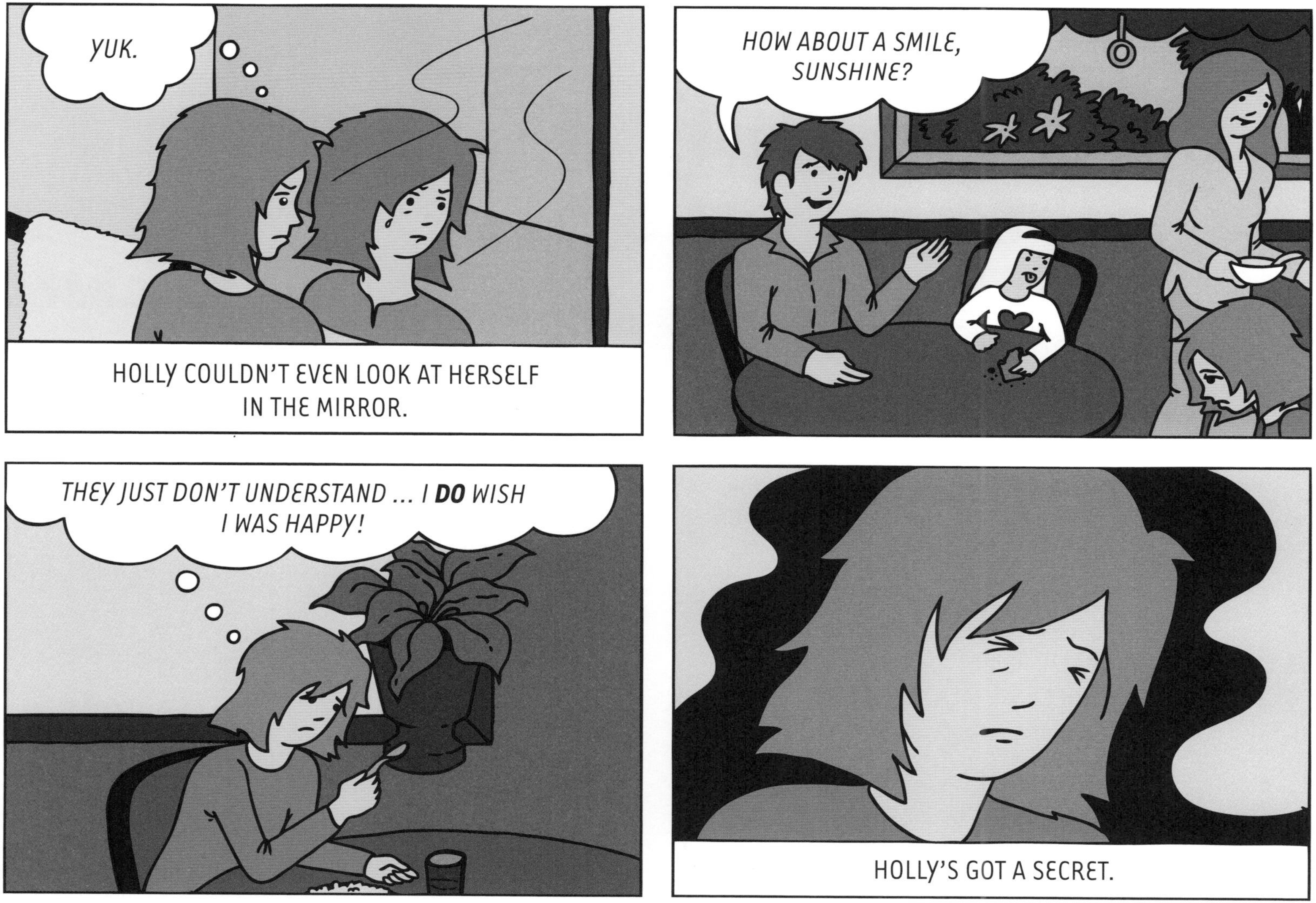
YUK.
HOLLY COULDN'T EVEN LOOK AT HERSELF IN THE MIRROR.
HOW ABOUT A SMILE, SUNSHINE?
THEY JUST DON'T UNDERSTAND ... I **DO** WISH I WAS HAPPY!
HOLLY'S GOT A SECRET.

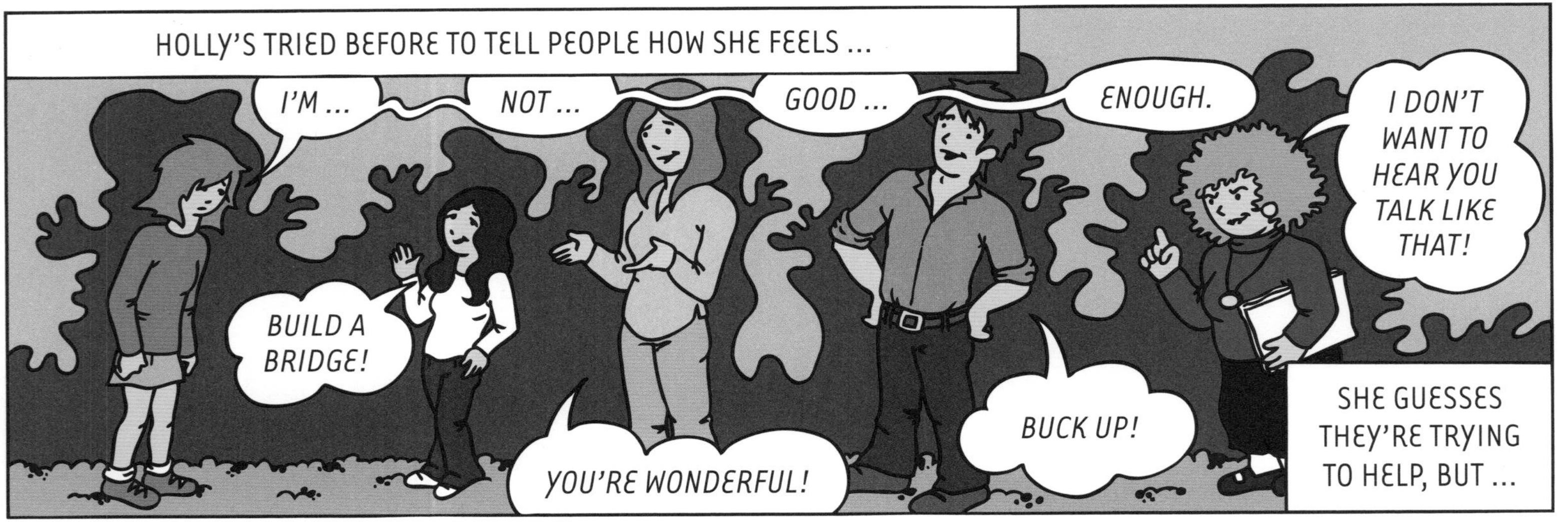
HOLLY'S TRIED BEFORE TO TELL PEOPLE HOW SHE FEELS ...
I'M ...
NOT ...
GOOD ...
ENOUGH.
I DON'T WANT TO HEAR YOU TALK LIKE THAT!
BUILD A BRIDGE!
YOU'RE WONDERFUL!
BUCK UP!
SHE GUESSES THEY'RE TRYING TO HELP, BUT ...

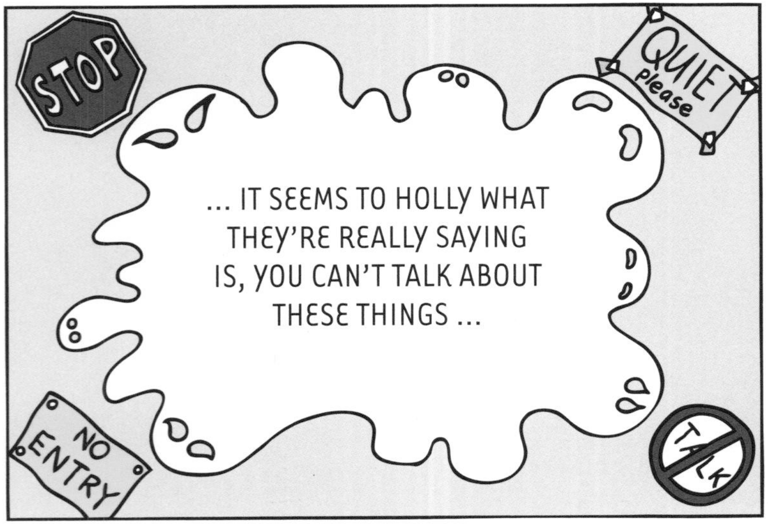
STOP
QUIET please
... IT SEEMS TO HOLLY WHAT THEY'RE REALLY SAYING IS, YOU CAN'T TALK ABOUT THESE THINGS ...
NO ENTRY
TALK

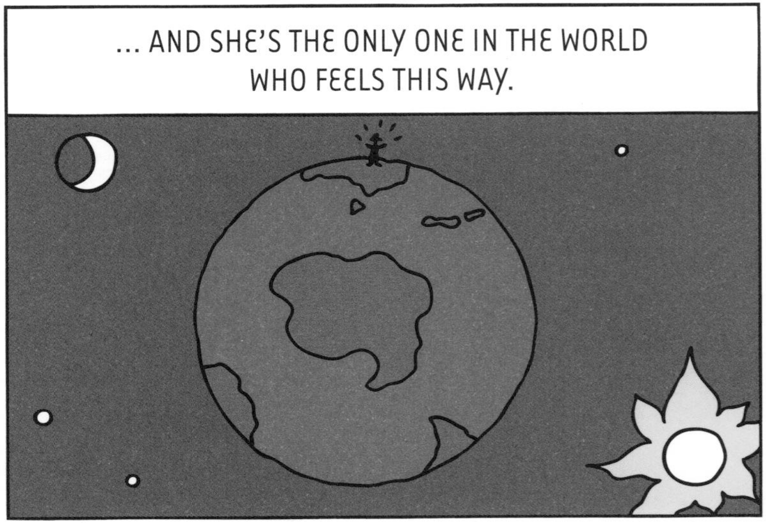
... AND SHE'S THE ONLY ONE IN THE WORLD WHO FEELS THIS WAY.

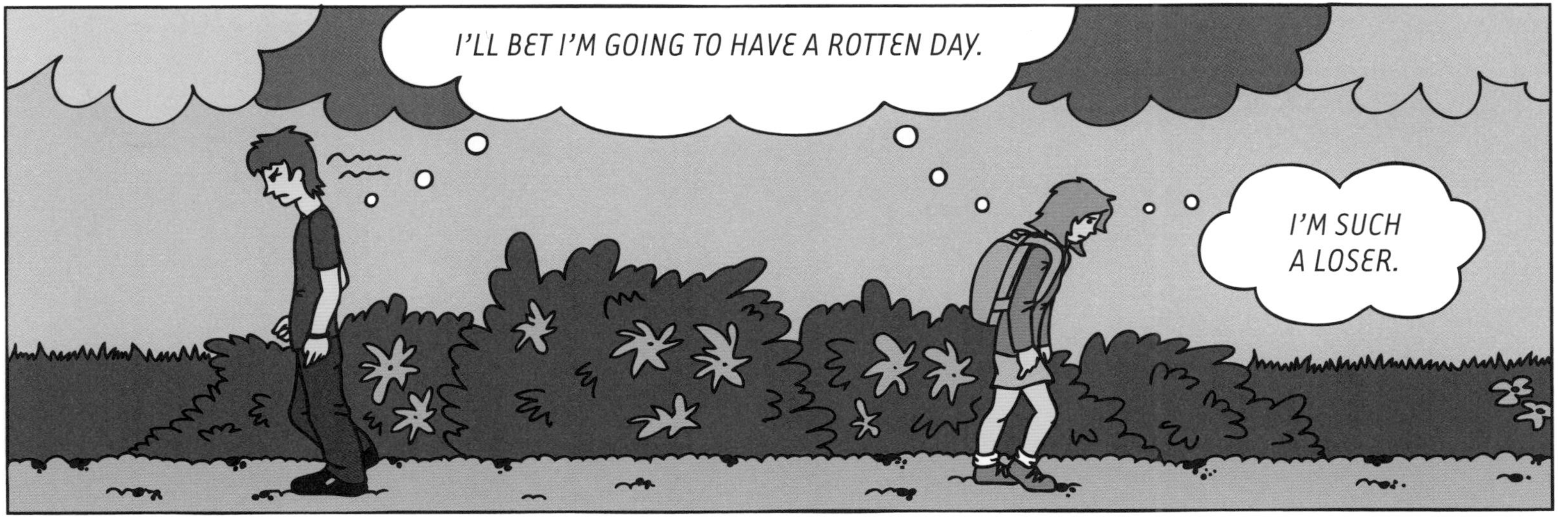

I'LL BET I'M GOING TO HAVE A ROTTEN DAY.
I'M SUCH A LOSER.

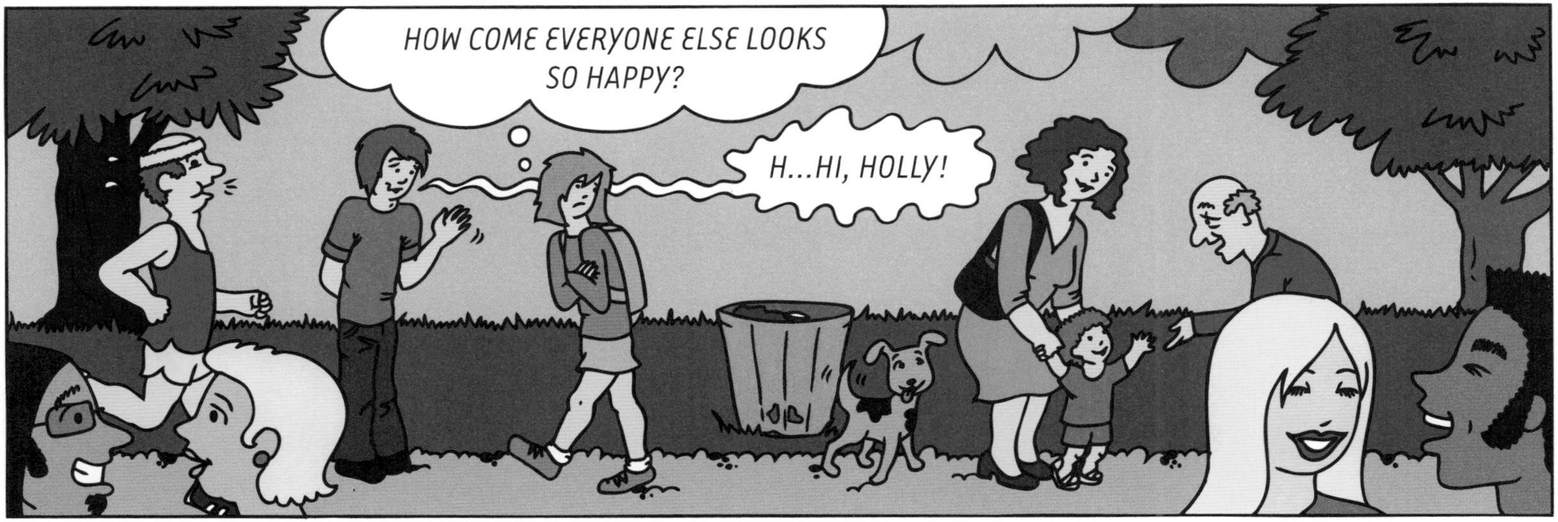

HOW COME EVERYONE ELSE LOOKS SO HAPPY?
H...HI, HOLLY!

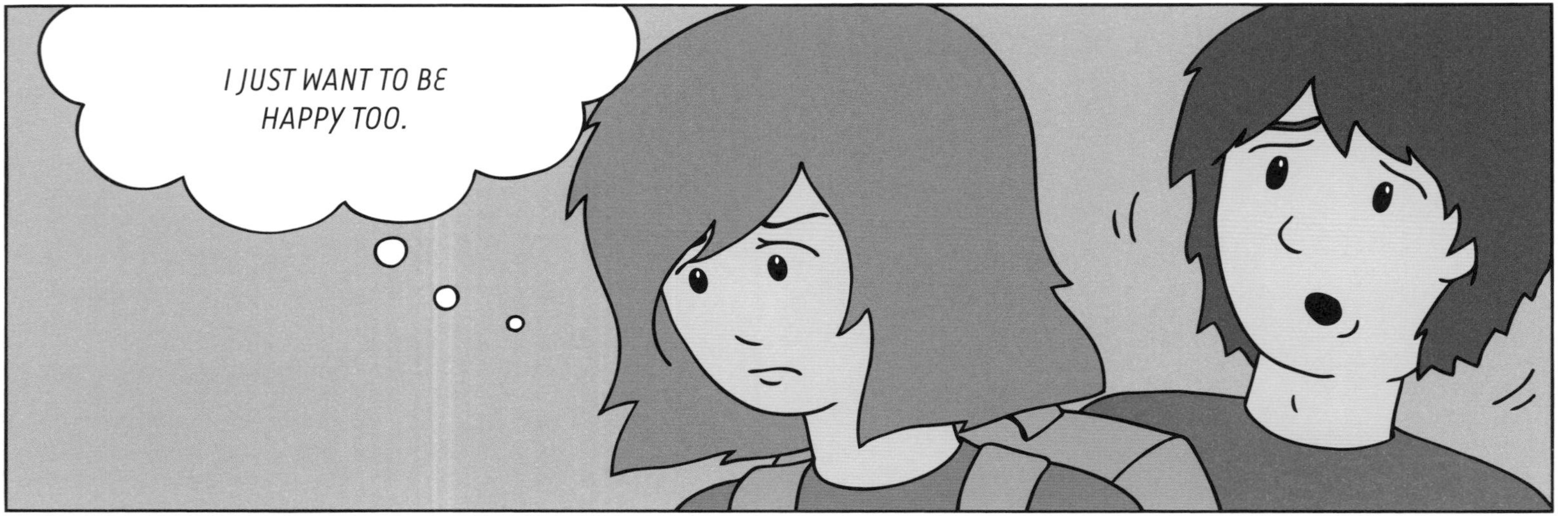
I JUST WANT TO BE
HAPPY TOO.

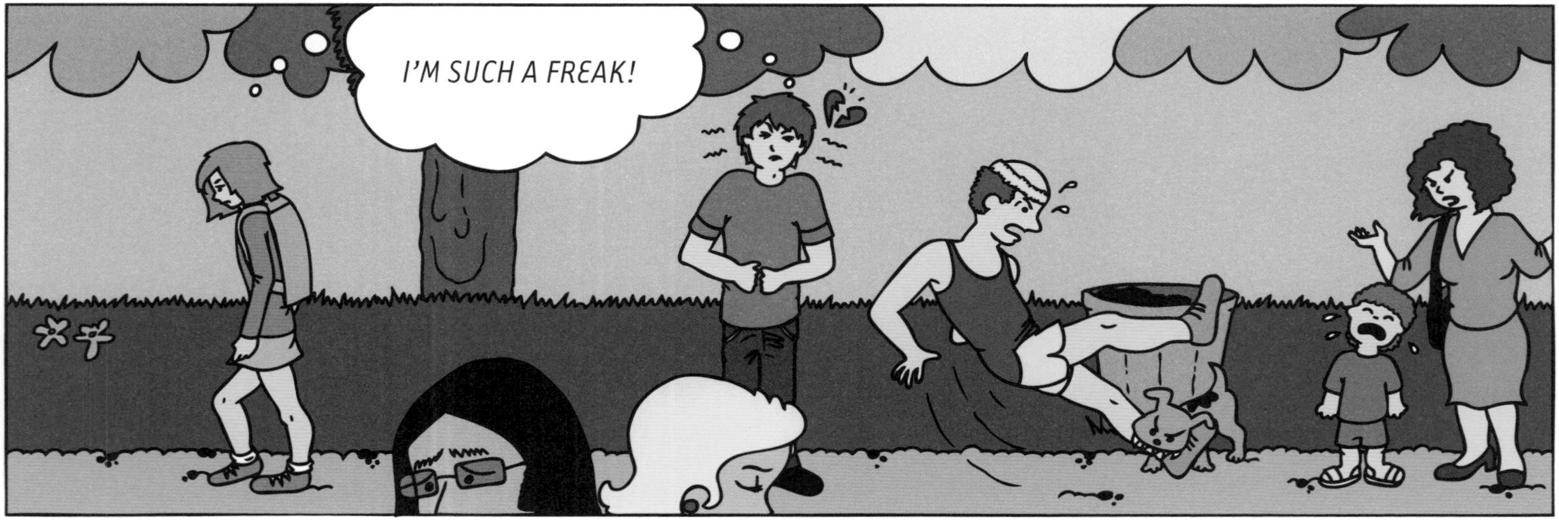
I'M SUCH A FREAK!

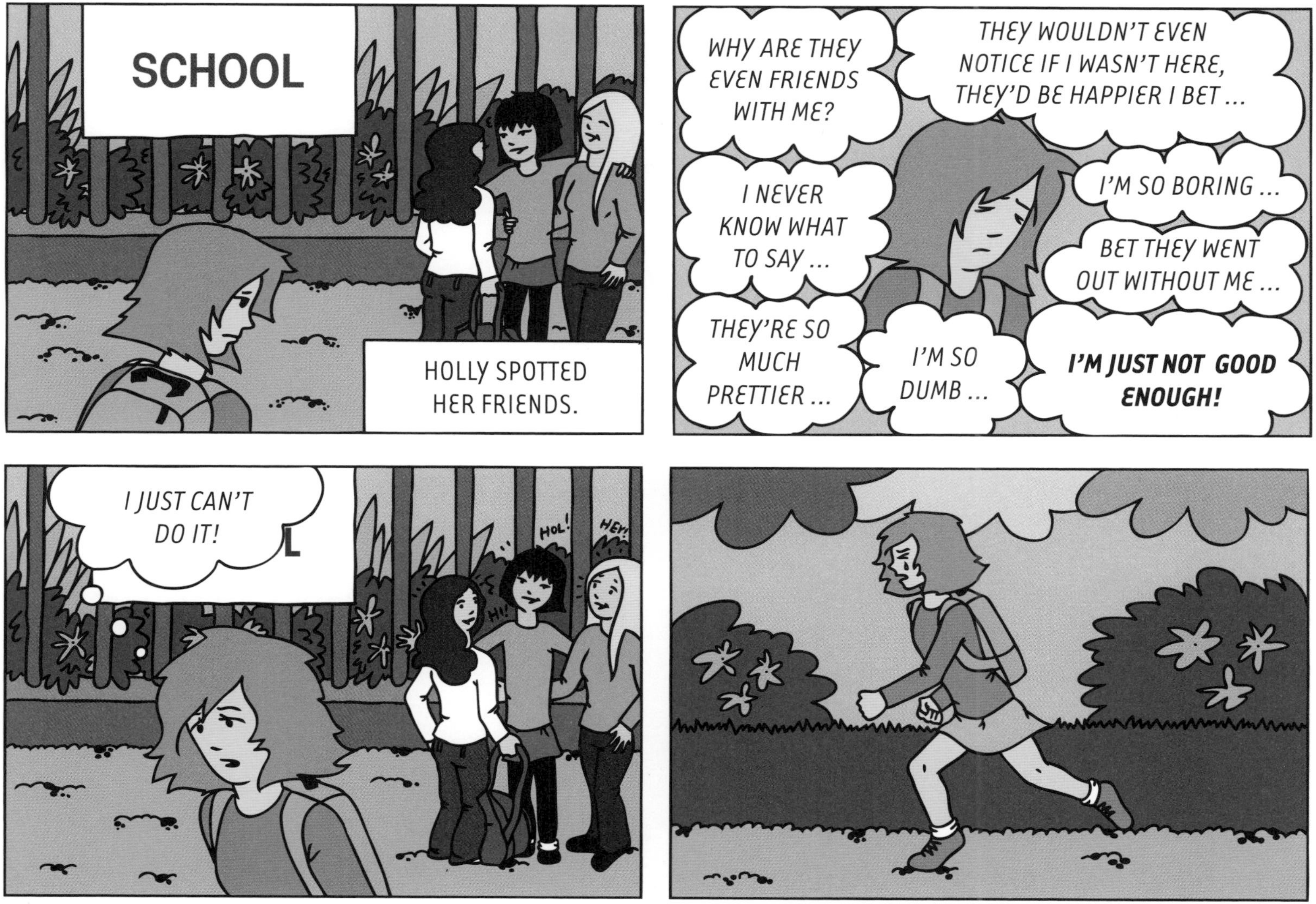
SCHOOL
HOLLY SPOTTED HER FRIENDS.
WHY ARE THEY EVEN FRIENDS WITH ME?
THEY WOULDN'T EVEN NOTICE IF I WASN'T HERE, THEY'D BE HAPPIER I BET ...
I NEVER KNOW WHAT TO SAY ...
I'M SO BORING ...
BET THEY WENT OUT WITHOUT ME ...
THEY'RE SO MUCH PRETTIER ...
I'M SO DUMB ...
I'M JUST NOT GOOD ENOUGH!
I JUST CAN'T DO IT!
HOL!
HEY!
HI!

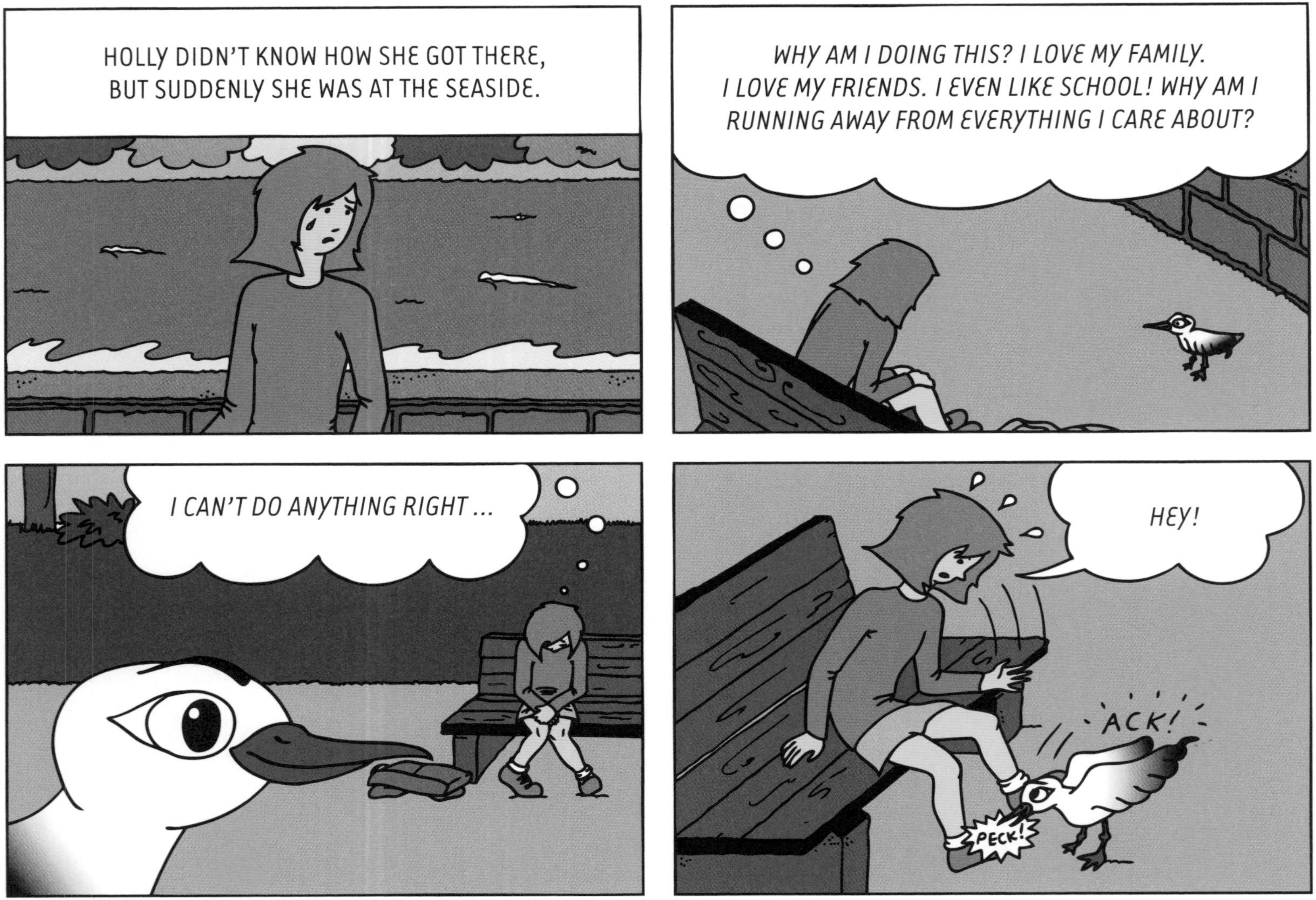
HOLLY DIDN'T KNOW HOW SHE GOT THERE, BUT SUDDENLY SHE WAS AT THE SEASIDE.
WHY AM I DOING THIS? I LOVE MY FAMILY. I LOVE MY FRIENDS. I EVEN LIKE SCHOOL! WHY AM I RUNNING AWAY FROM EVERYTHING I CARE ABOUT?
I CAN'T DO ANYTHING RIGHT ...
HEY!
ACK!
PECK!

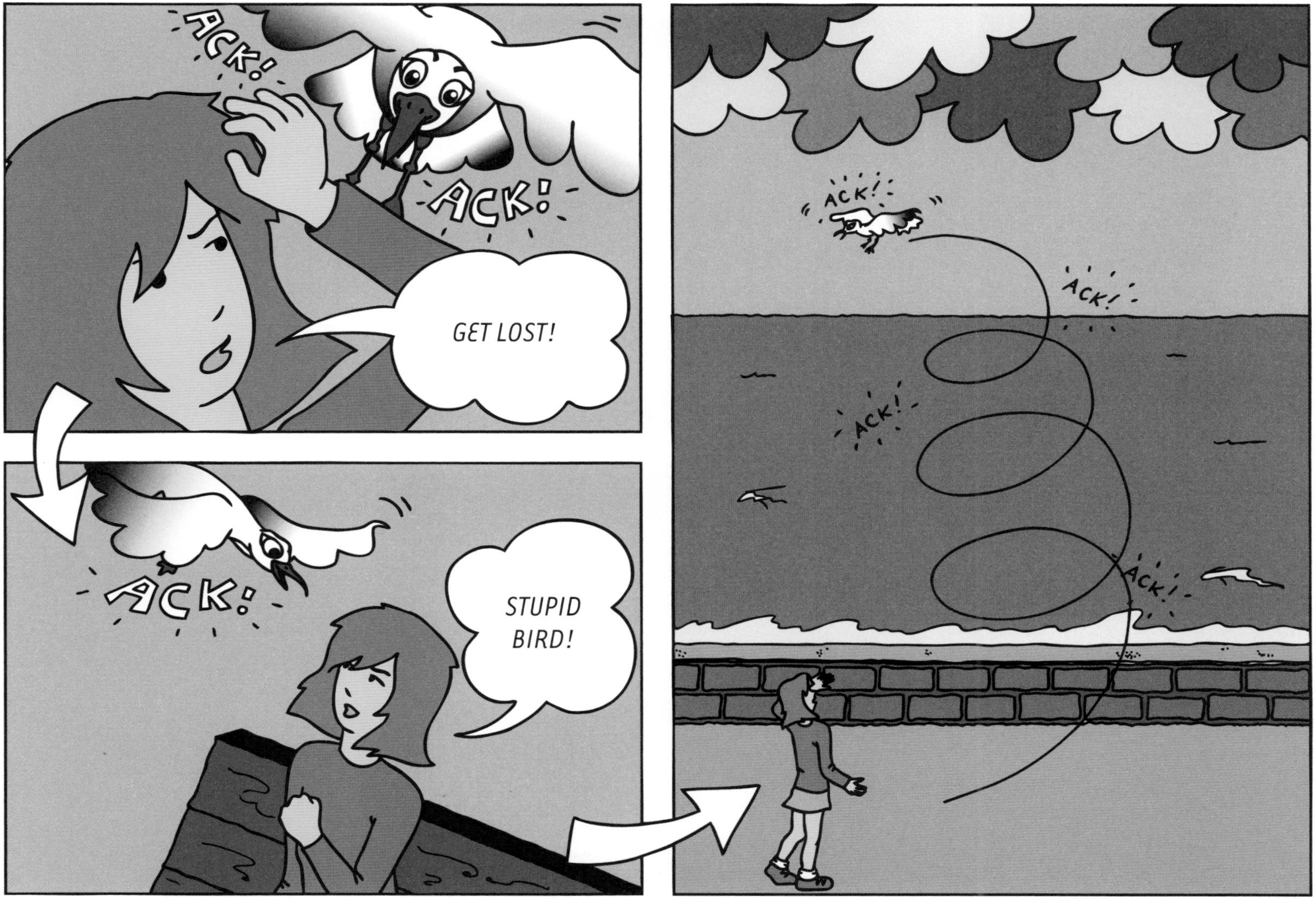
ACK!
ACK!
GET LOST!
ACK!
STUPID BIRD!
ACK!
ACK!
ACK!
ACK!

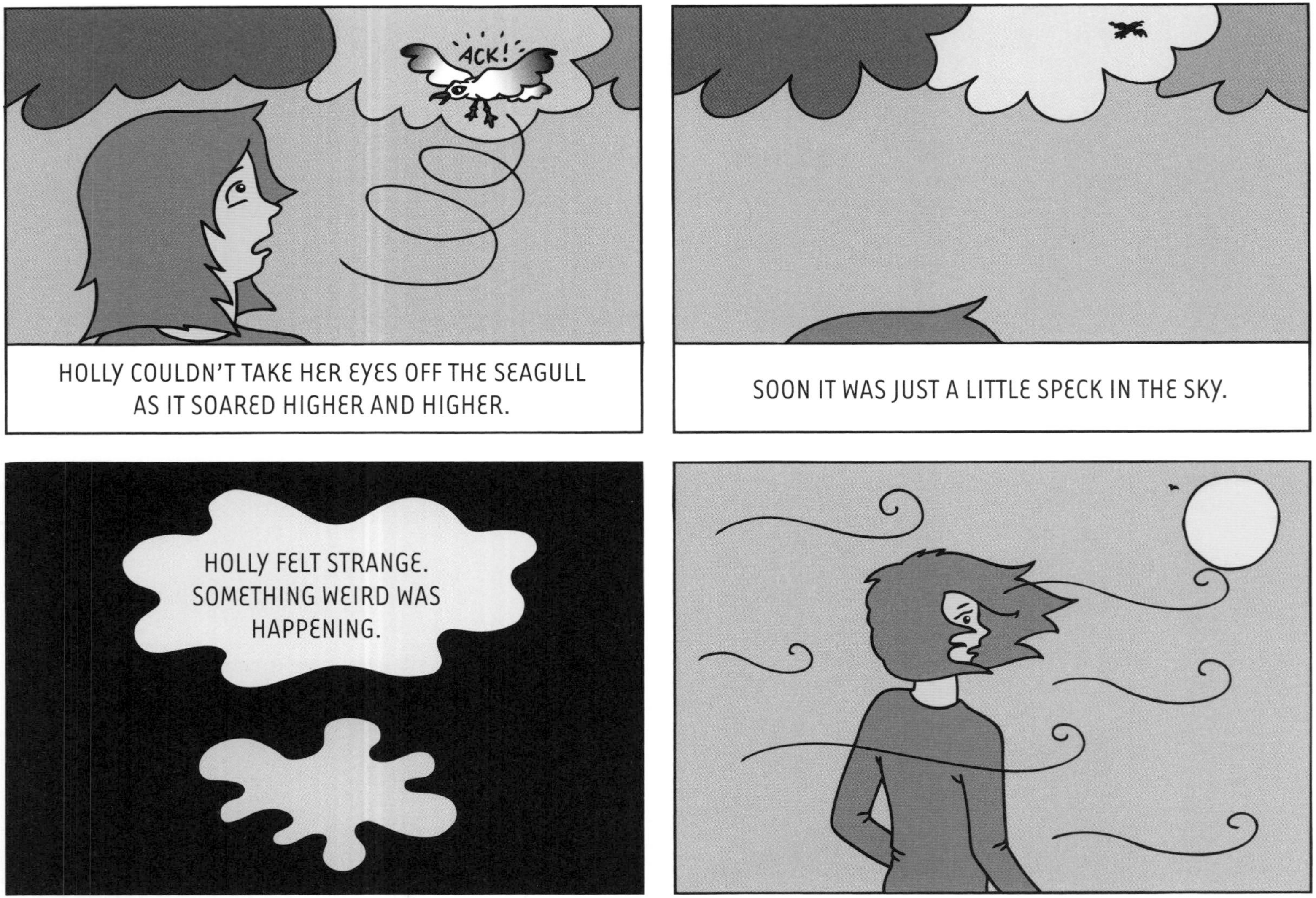
ACK!
HOLLY COULDN'T TAKE HER EYES OFF THE SEAGULL AS IT SOARED HIGHER AND HIGHER.
SOON IT WAS JUST A LITTLE SPECK IN THE SKY.
HOLLY FELT STRANGE. SOMETHING WEIRD WAS HAPPENING.

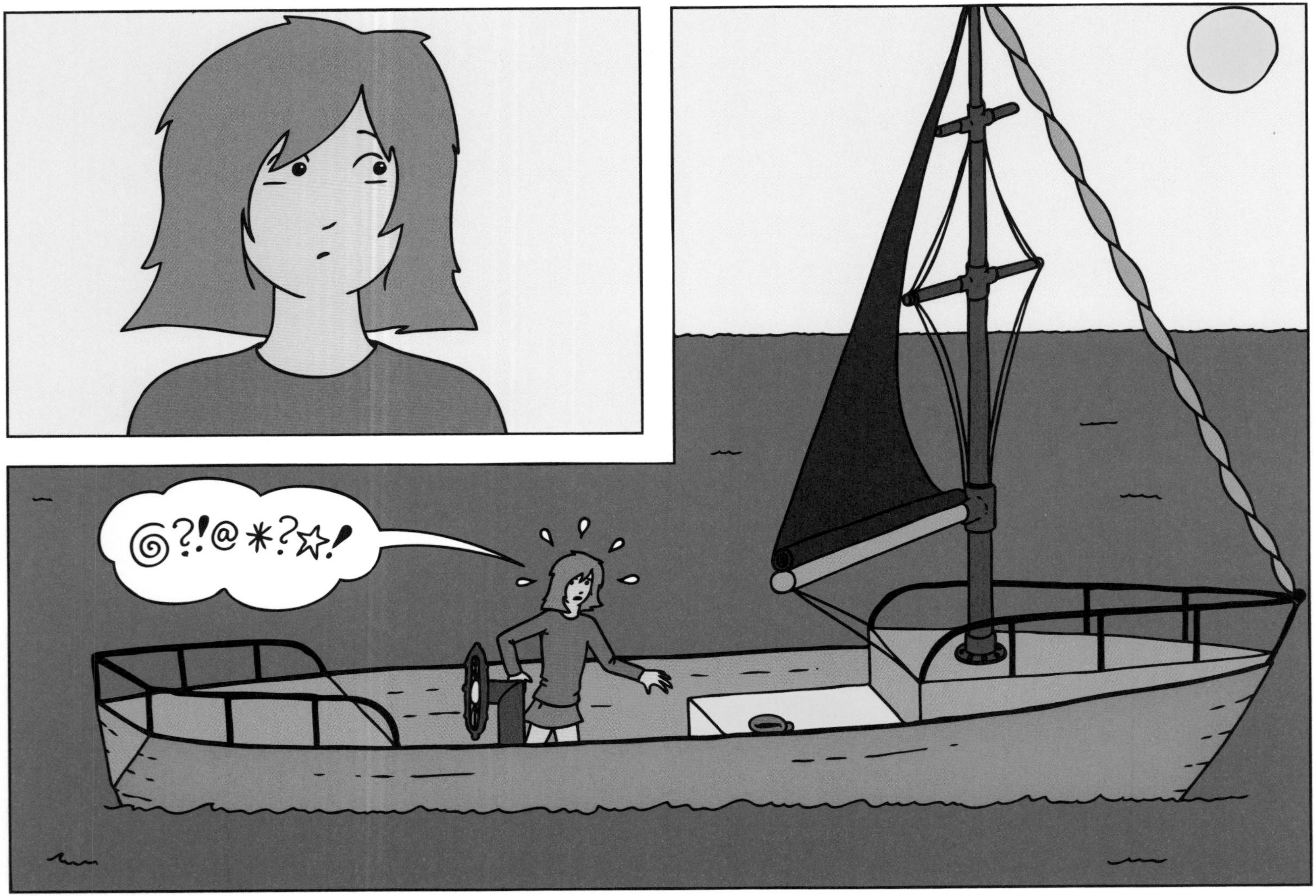

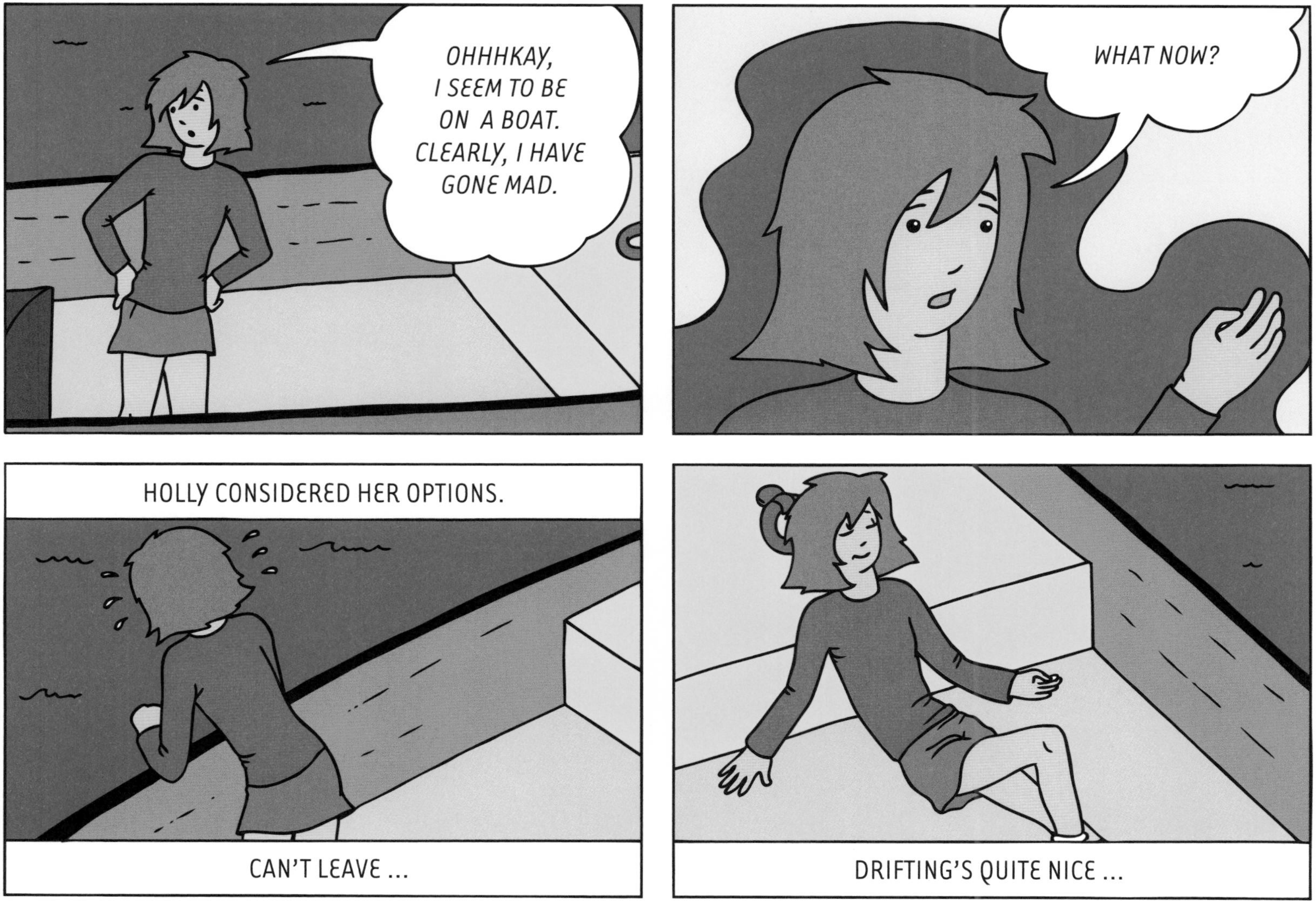
OHHHKAY, I SEEM TO BE ON A BOAT. CLEARLY, I HAVE GONE MAD.
WHAT NOW?
HOLLY CONSIDERED HER OPTIONS.
CAN'T LEAVE ...
DRIFTING'S QUITE NICE ...

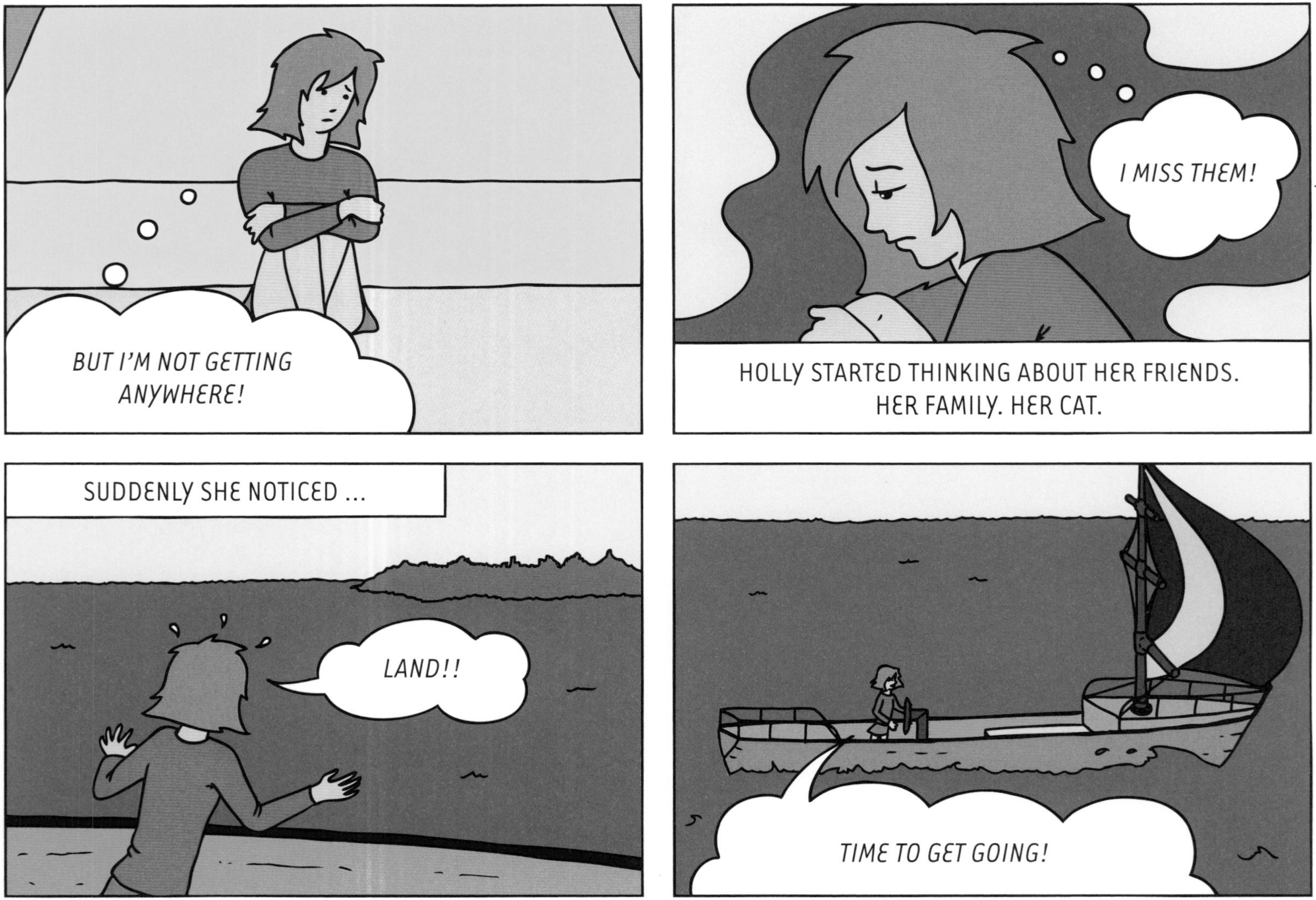
BUT I'M NOT GETTING ANYWHERE!
I MISS THEM!
HOLLY STARTED THINKING ABOUT HER FRIENDS. HER FAMILY. HER CAT.
SUDDENLY SHE NOTICED ...
LAND!!
TIME TO GET GOING!

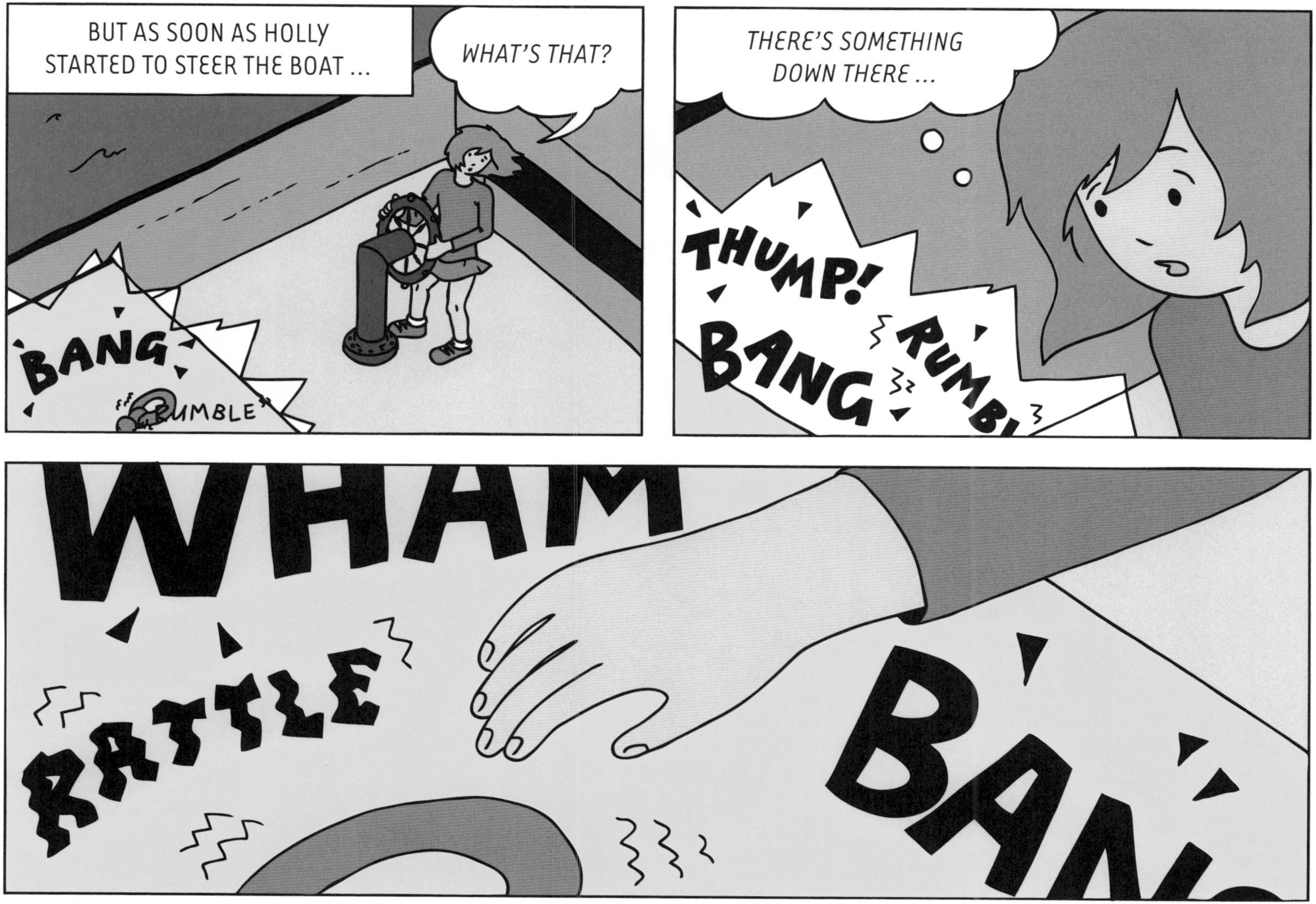
BUT AS SOON AS HOLLY STARTED TO STEER THE BOAT ...
WHAT'S THAT?
BANG
RUMBLE
THERE'S SOMETHING DOWN THERE ...
THUMP!
BANG
RUMB
WHAM
RATTLE
BAN

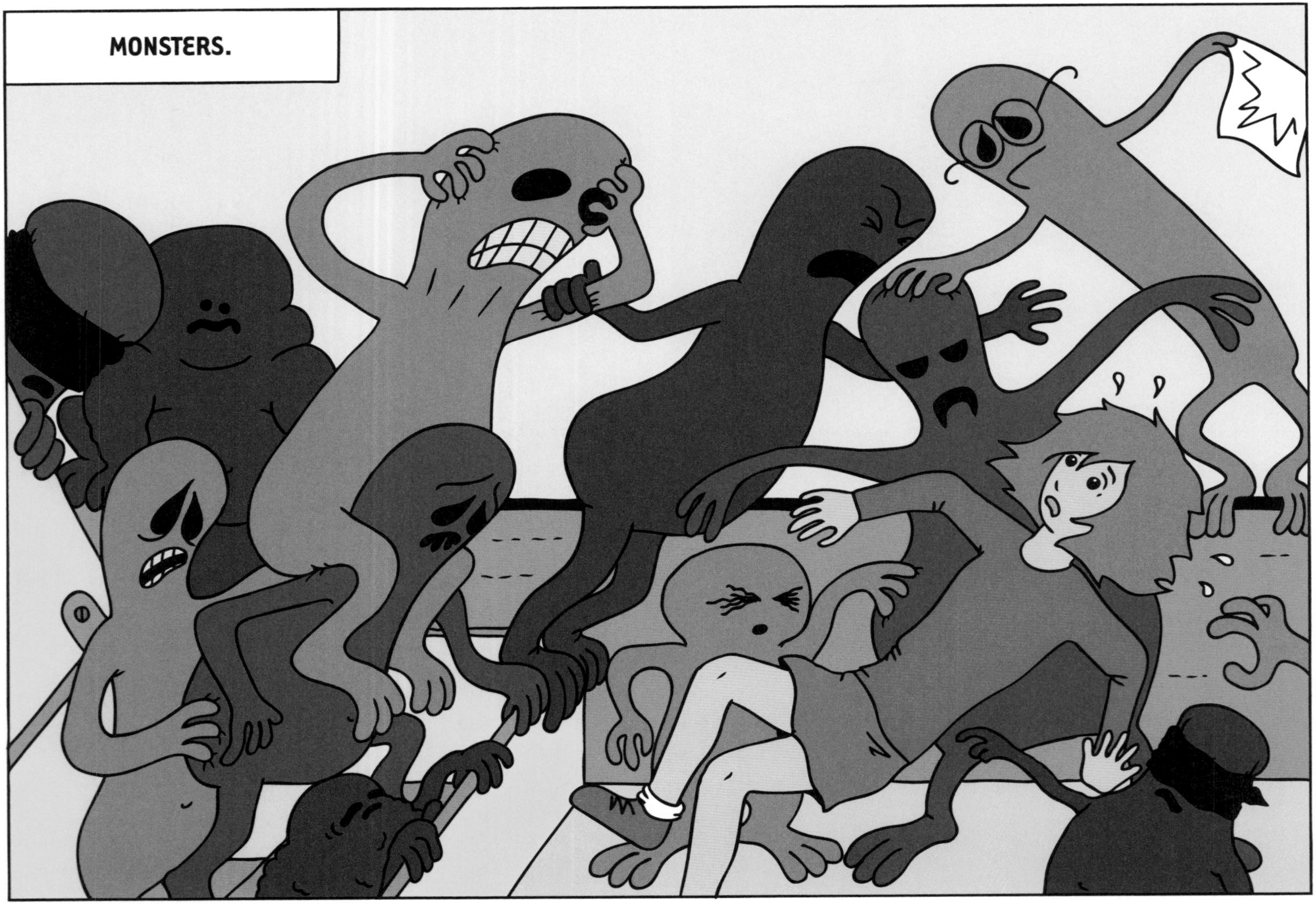
MONSTERS.

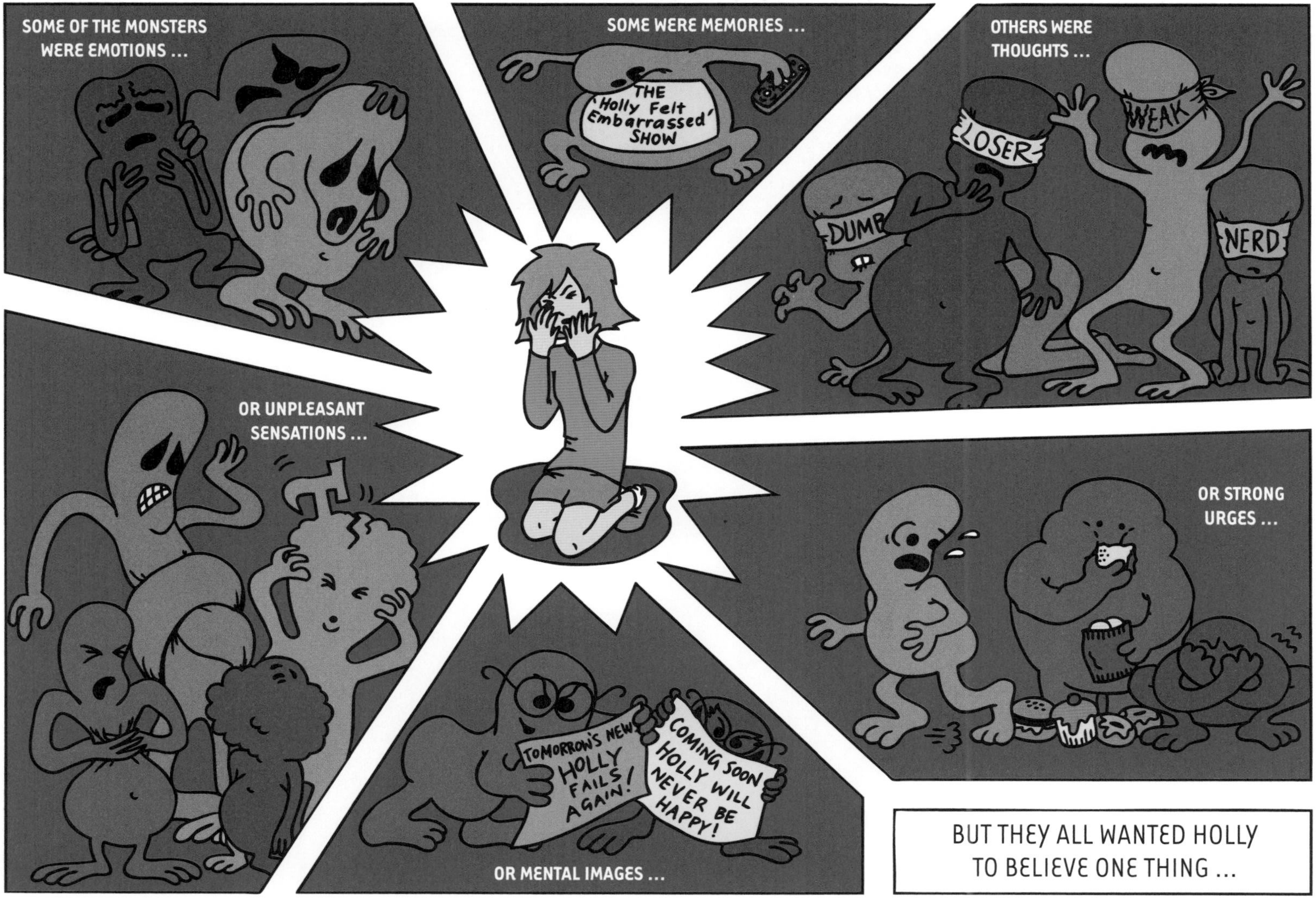
SOME OF THE MONSTERS WERE EMOTIONS ...
SOME WERE MEMORIES ...
THE 'Holly Felt Embarrassed' SHOW
OTHERS WERE THOUGHTS ...
LOSER
WEAK
DUMB
NERD
OR UNPLEASANT SENSATIONS ...
OR STRONG URGES ...
TOMORROW'S NEWS HOLLY FAILS AGAIN!
COMING SOON HOLLY WILL NEVER BE HAPPY!
OR MENTAL IMAGES ...

BUT THEY ALL WANTED HOLLY TO BELIEVE ONE THING ...

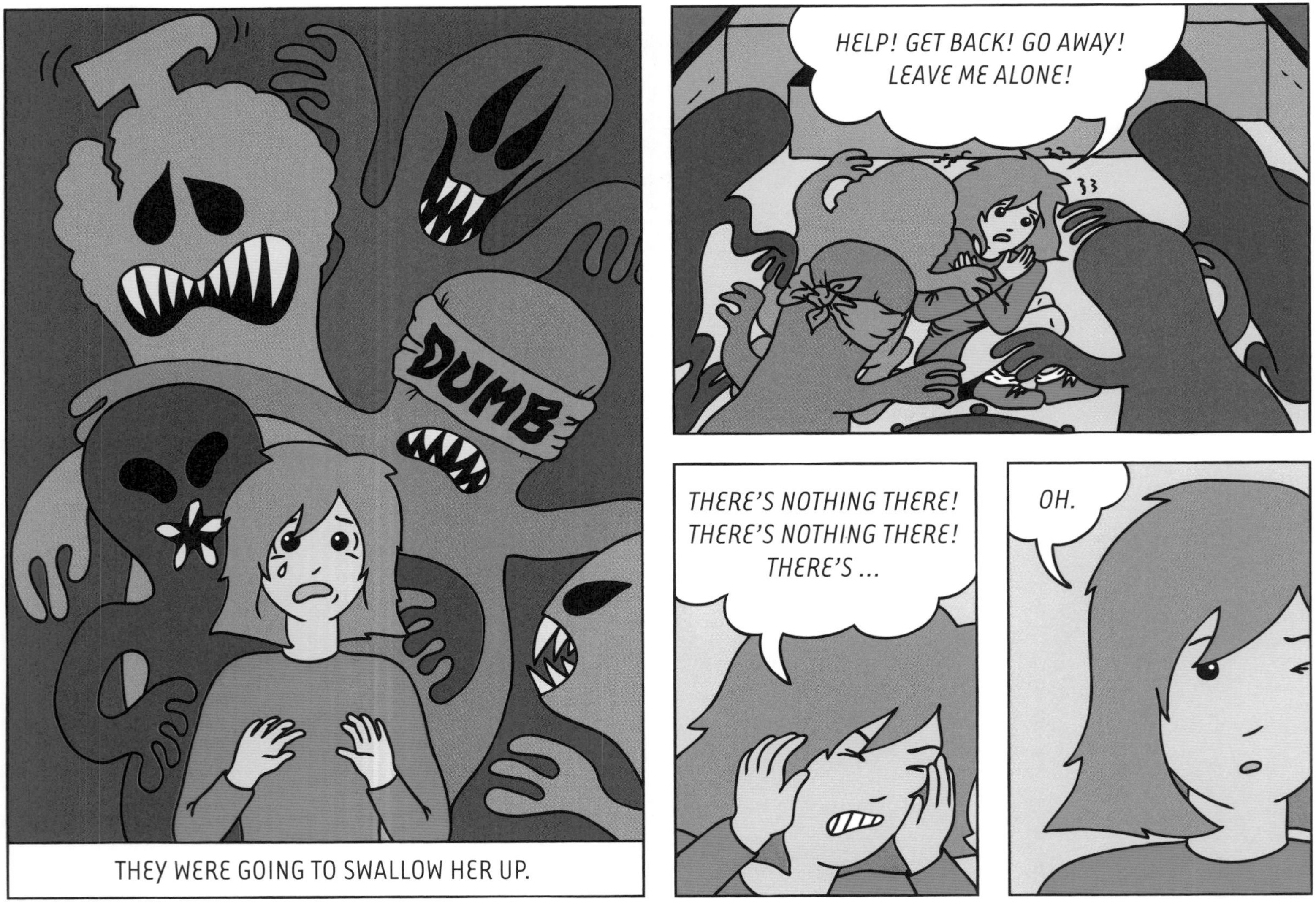
DUMB
THEY WERE GOING TO SWALLOW HER UP.
HELP! GET BACK! GO AWAY! LEAVE ME ALONE!
THERE'S NOTHING THERE! THERE'S NOTHING THERE! THERE'S ...
OH.

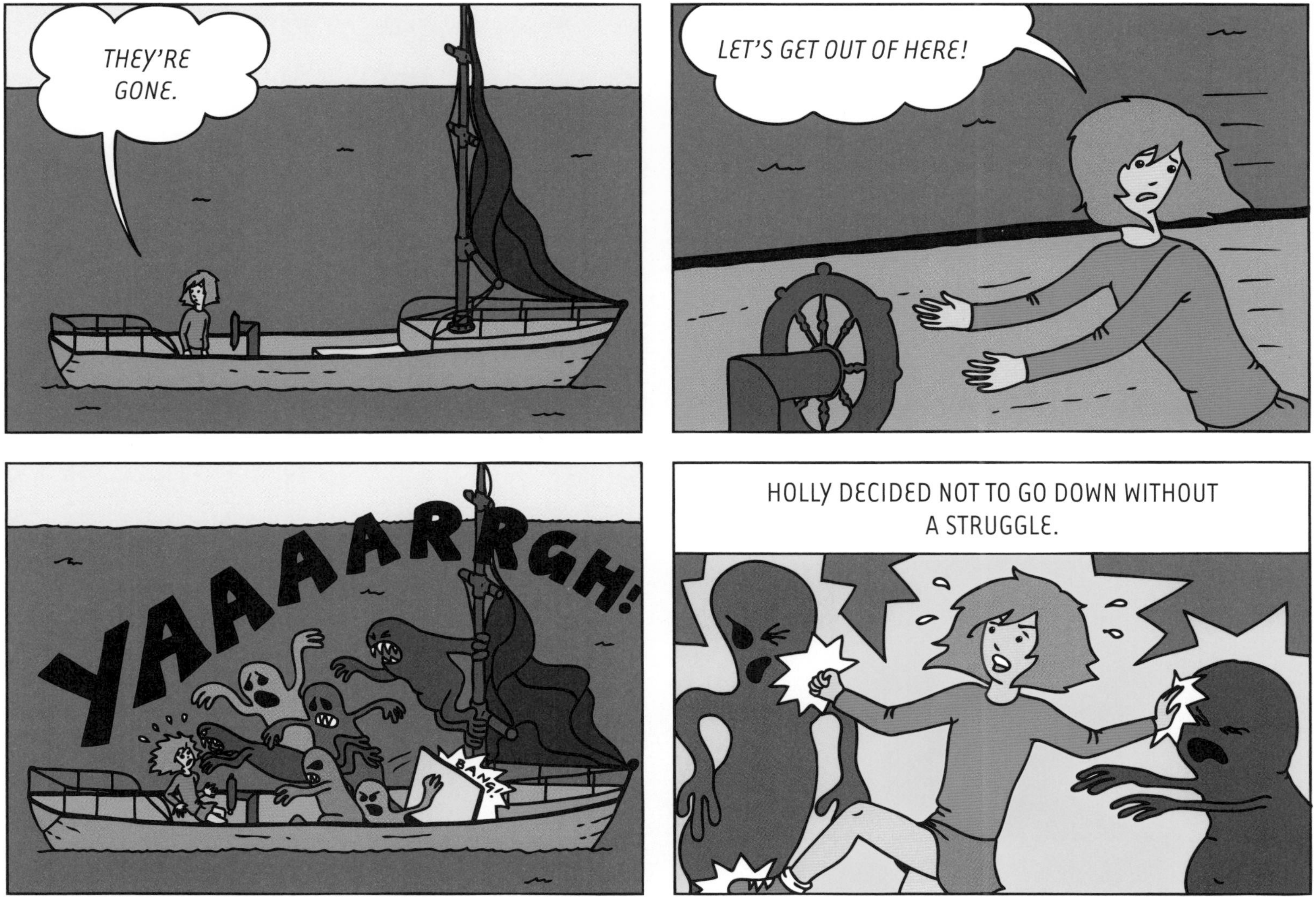
THEY'RE GONE.
LET'S GET OUT OF HERE!
YAAAARRGH!
BANG!
HOLLY DECIDED NOT TO GO DOWN WITHOUT A STRUGGLE.

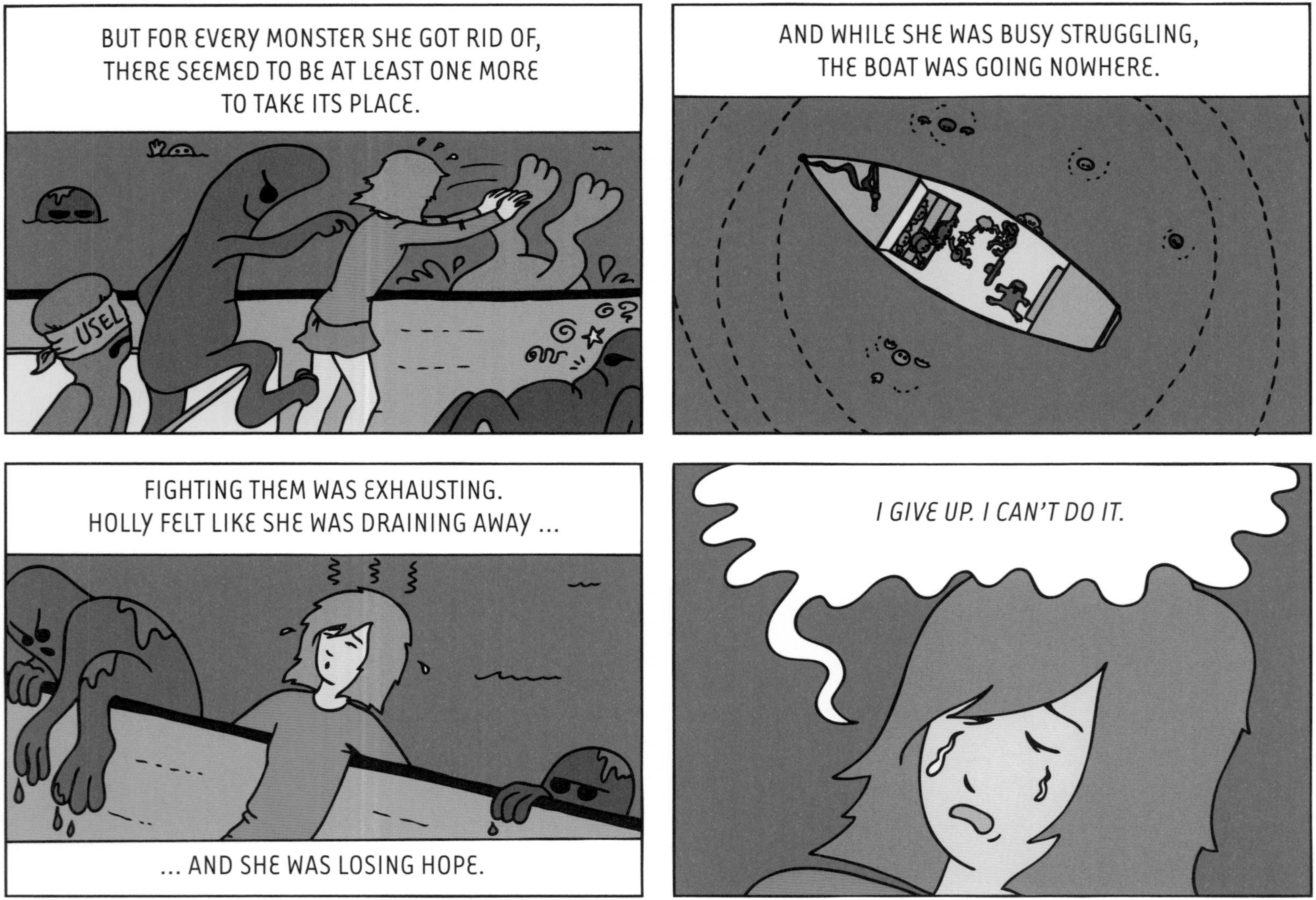
BUT FOR EVERY MONSTER SHE GOT RID OF, THERE SEEMED TO BE AT LEAST ONE MORE TO TAKE ITS PLACE.
USEL
AND WHILE SHE WAS BUSY STRUGGLING, THE BOAT WAS GOING NOWHERE.
FIGHTING THEM WAS EXHAUSTING. HOLLY FELT LIKE SHE WAS DRAINING AWAY ...
... AND SHE WAS LOSING HOPE.
I GIVE UP. I CAN'T DO IT.

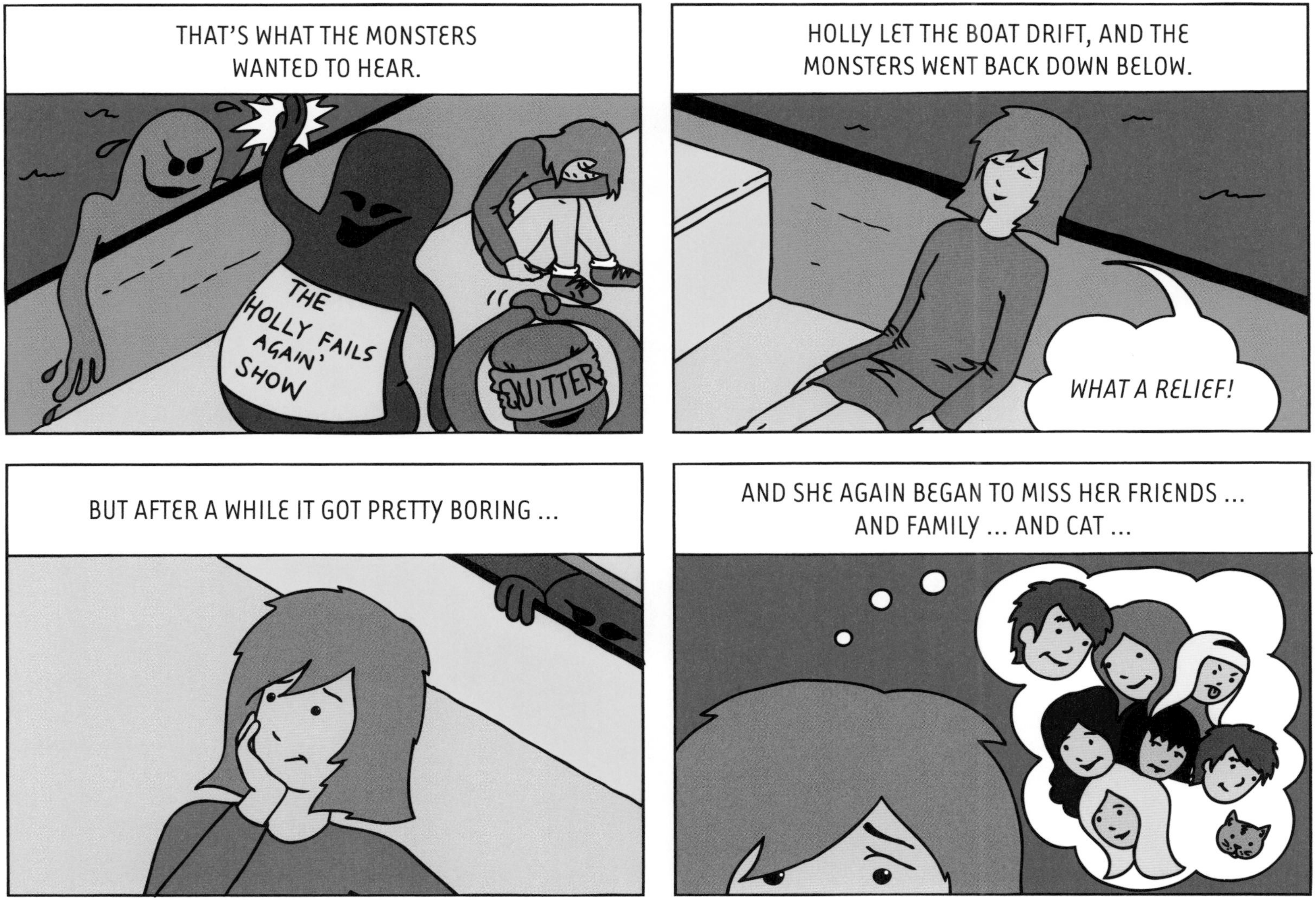
THAT'S WHAT THE MONSTERS WANTED TO HEAR.
THE 'HOLLY FAILS AGAIN' SHOW
QUITTER
HOLLY LET THE BOAT DRIFT, AND THE MONSTERS WENT BACK DOWN BELOW.
WHAT A RELIEF!
BUT AFTER A WHILE IT GOT PRETTY BORING ...
AND SHE AGAIN BEGAN TO MISS HER FRIENDS ... AND FAMILY ... AND CAT ...

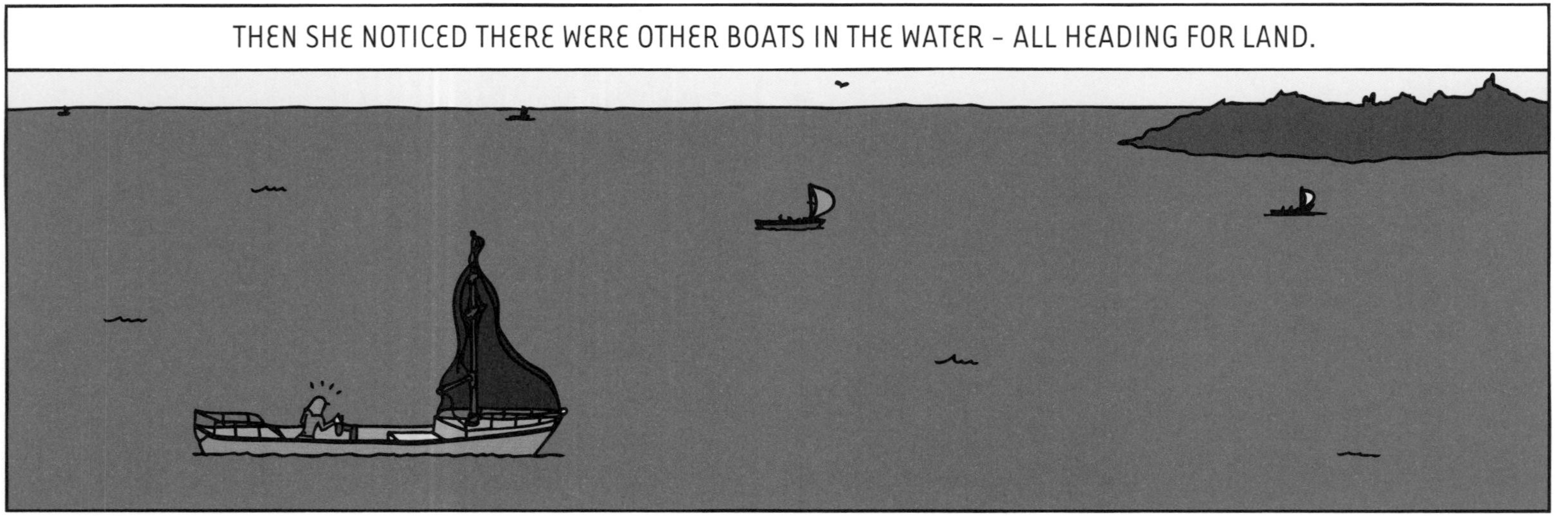
THEN SHE NOTICED THERE WERE OTHER BOATS IN THE WATER – ALL HEADING FOR LAND.

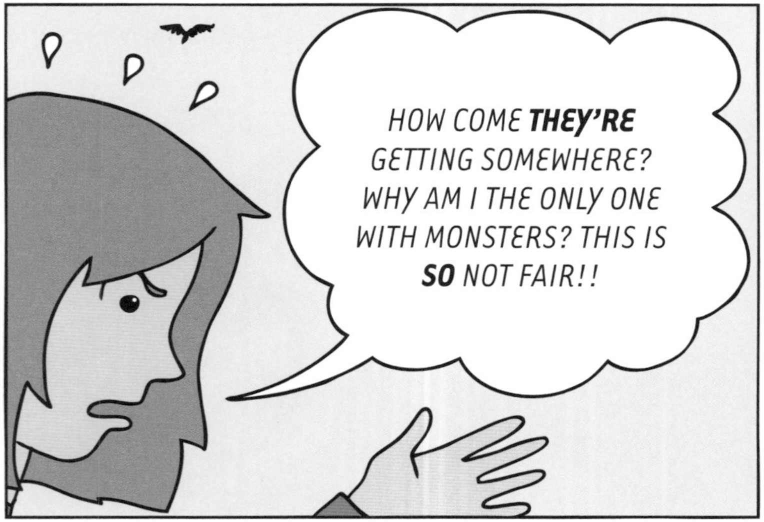
*HOW COME **THEY'RE** GETTING SOMEWHERE? WHY AM I THE ONLY ONE WITH MONSTERS? THIS IS **SO** NOT FAIR!!*

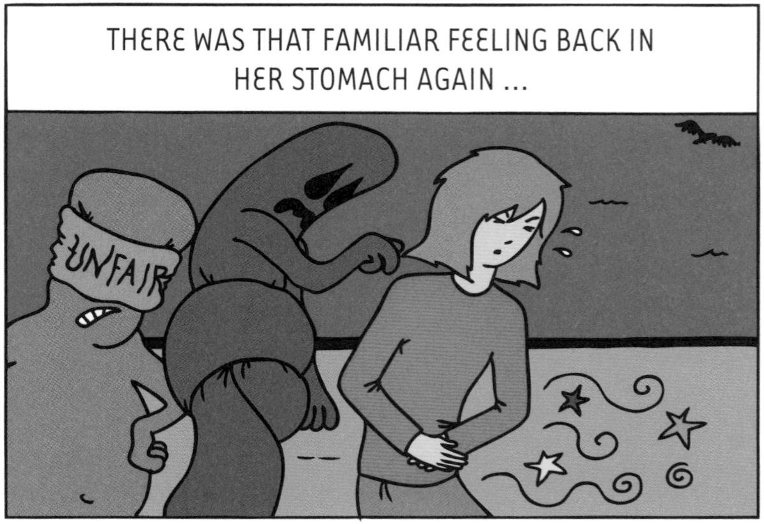
THERE WAS THAT FAMILIAR FEELING BACK IN HER STOMACH AGAIN ...
UNFAIR

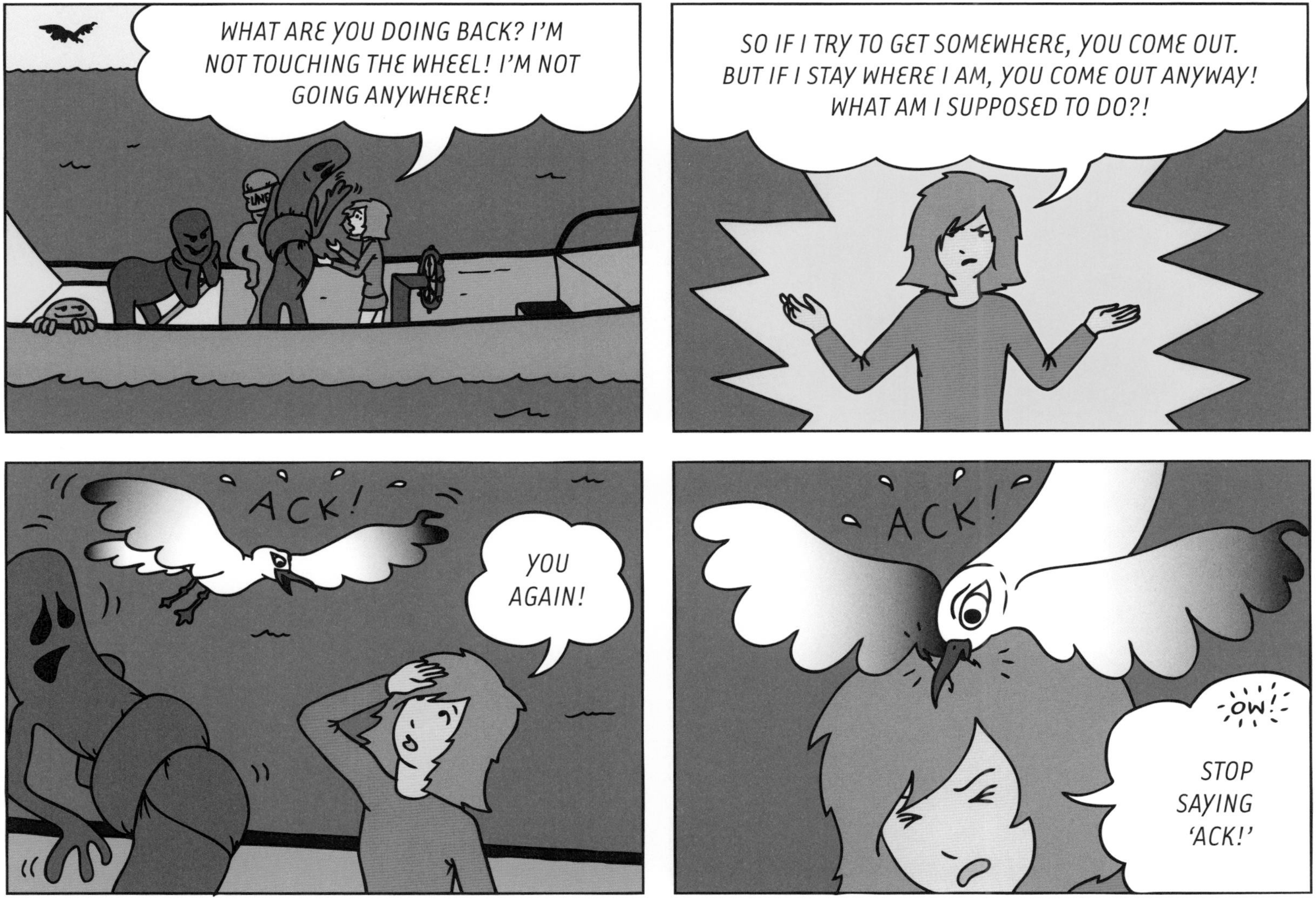

WHAT ARE YOU DOING BACK? I'M NOT TOUCHING THE WHEEL! I'M NOT GOING ANYWHERE!
SO IF I TRY TO GET SOMEWHERE, YOU COME OUT. BUT IF I STAY WHERE I AM, YOU COME OUT ANYWAY! WHAT AM I SUPPOSED TO DO?!
ACK!
YOU AGAIN!
ACK!
OW!
STOP SAYING 'ACK!'

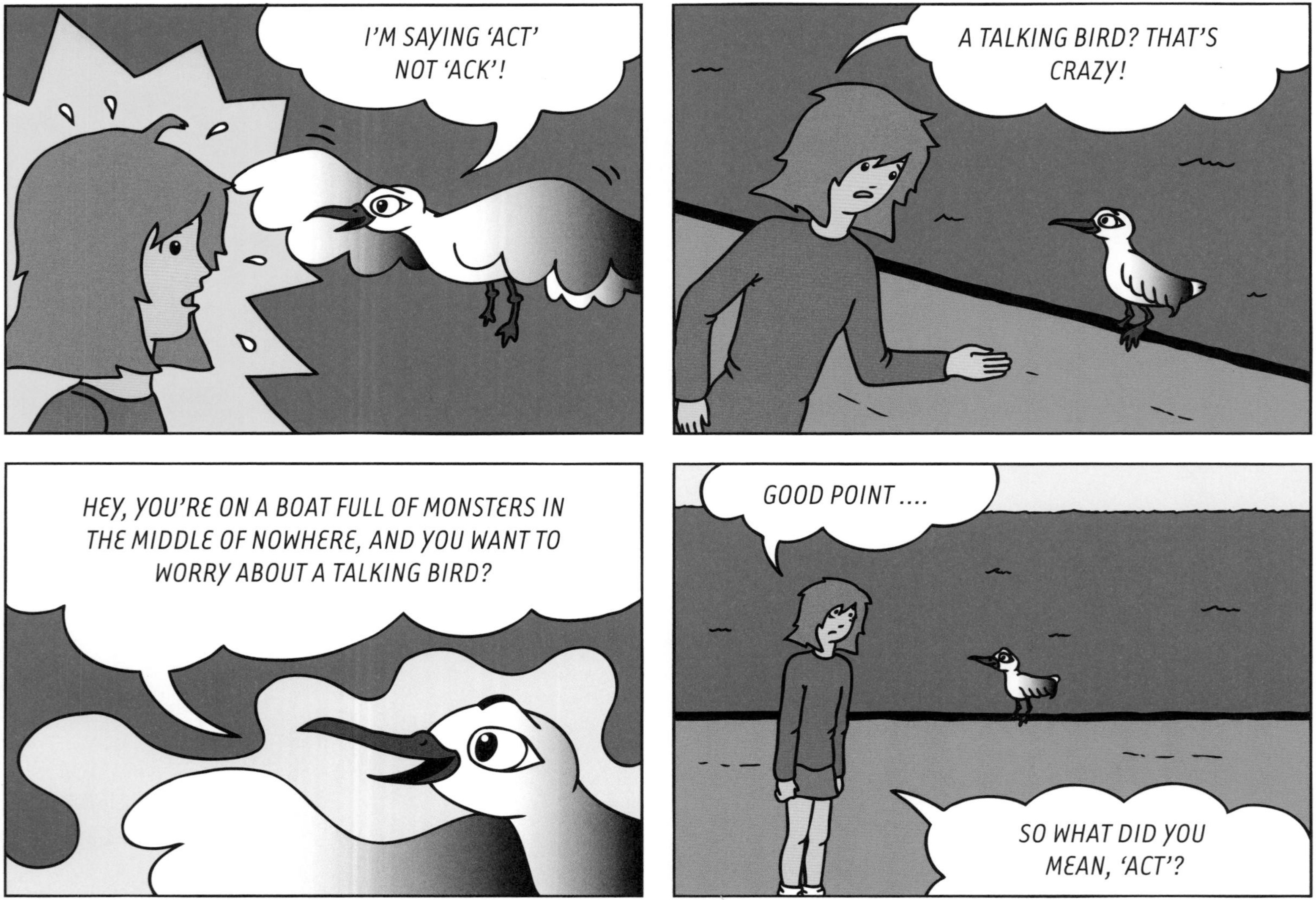
I'M SAYING 'ACT' NOT 'ACK'!
A TALKING BIRD? THAT'S CRAZY!
HEY, YOU'RE ON A BOAT FULL OF MONSTERS IN THE MIDDLE OF NOWHERE, AND YOU WANT TO WORRY ABOUT A TALKING BIRD?
GOOD POINT ....
SO WHAT DID YOU MEAN, 'ACT'?

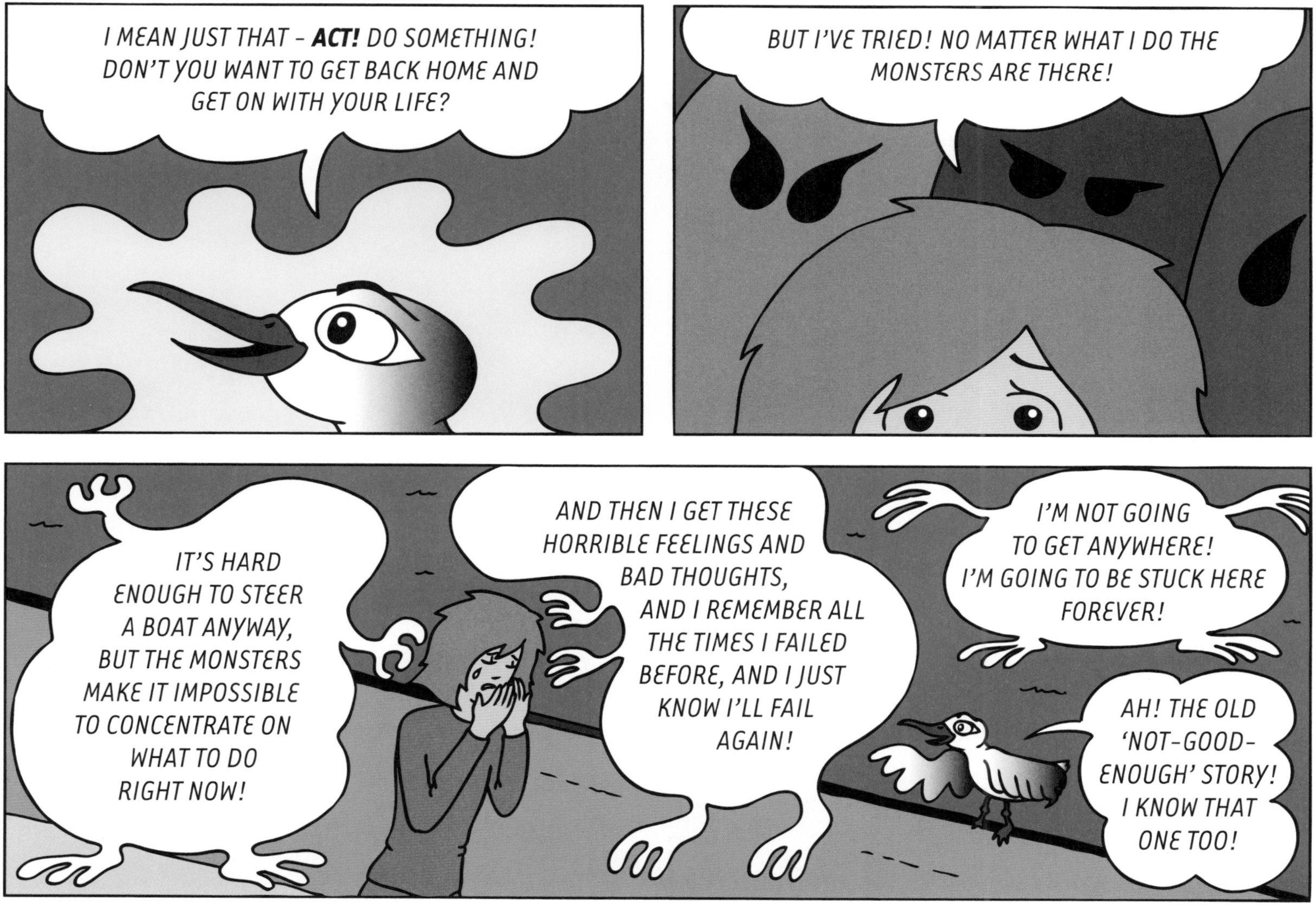
I MEAN JUST THAT – **ACT!** DO SOMETHING! DON'T YOU WANT TO GET BACK HOME AND GET ON WITH YOUR LIFE?
BUT I'VE TRIED! NO MATTER WHAT I DO THE MONSTERS ARE THERE!
IT'S HARD ENOUGH TO STEER A BOAT ANYWAY, BUT THE MONSTERS MAKE IT IMPOSSIBLE TO CONCENTRATE ON WHAT TO DO RIGHT NOW!
AND THEN I GET THESE HORRIBLE FEELINGS AND BAD THOUGHTS, AND I REMEMBER ALL THE TIMES I FAILED BEFORE, AND I JUST KNOW I'LL FAIL AGAIN!
I'M NOT GOING TO GET ANYWHERE! I'M GOING TO BE STUCK HERE FOREVER!
AH! THE OLD 'NOT-GOOD-ENOUGH' STORY! I KNOW THAT ONE TOO!

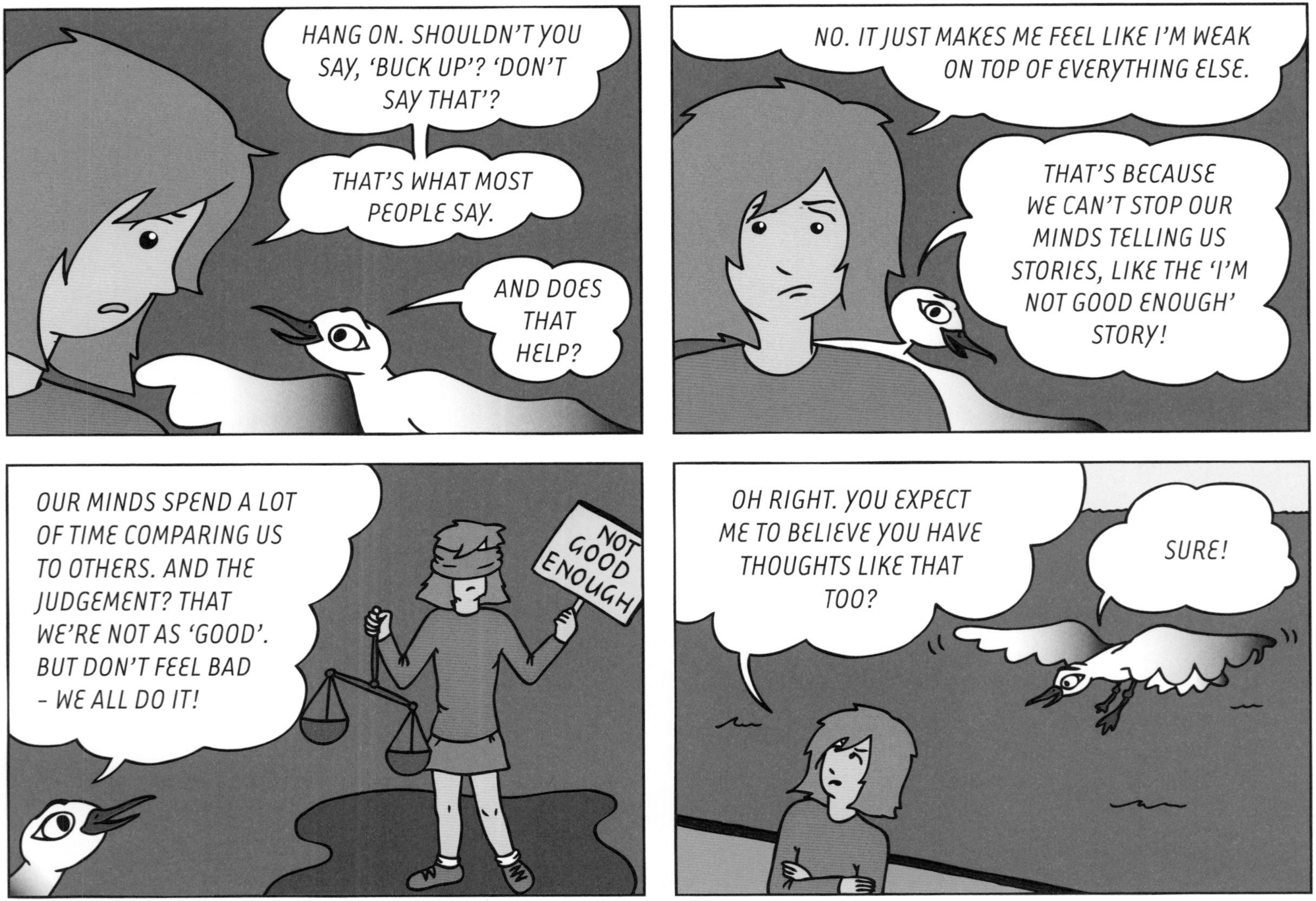
HANG ON. SHOULDN'T YOU SAY, 'BUCK UP'? 'DON'T SAY THAT'?
THAT'S WHAT MOST PEOPLE SAY.
AND DOES THAT HELP?
NO. IT JUST MAKES ME FEEL LIKE I'M WEAK ON TOP OF EVERYTHING ELSE.
THAT'S BECAUSE WE CAN'T STOP OUR MINDS TELLING US STORIES, LIKE THE 'I'M NOT GOOD ENOUGH' STORY!
OUR MINDS SPEND A LOT OF TIME COMPARING US TO OTHERS. AND THE JUDGEMENT? THAT WE'RE NOT AS 'GOOD'. BUT DON'T FEEL BAD – WE ALL DO IT!
NOT GOOD ENOUGH
OH RIGHT. YOU EXPECT ME TO BELIEVE YOU HAVE THOUGHTS LIKE THAT TOO?
SURE!

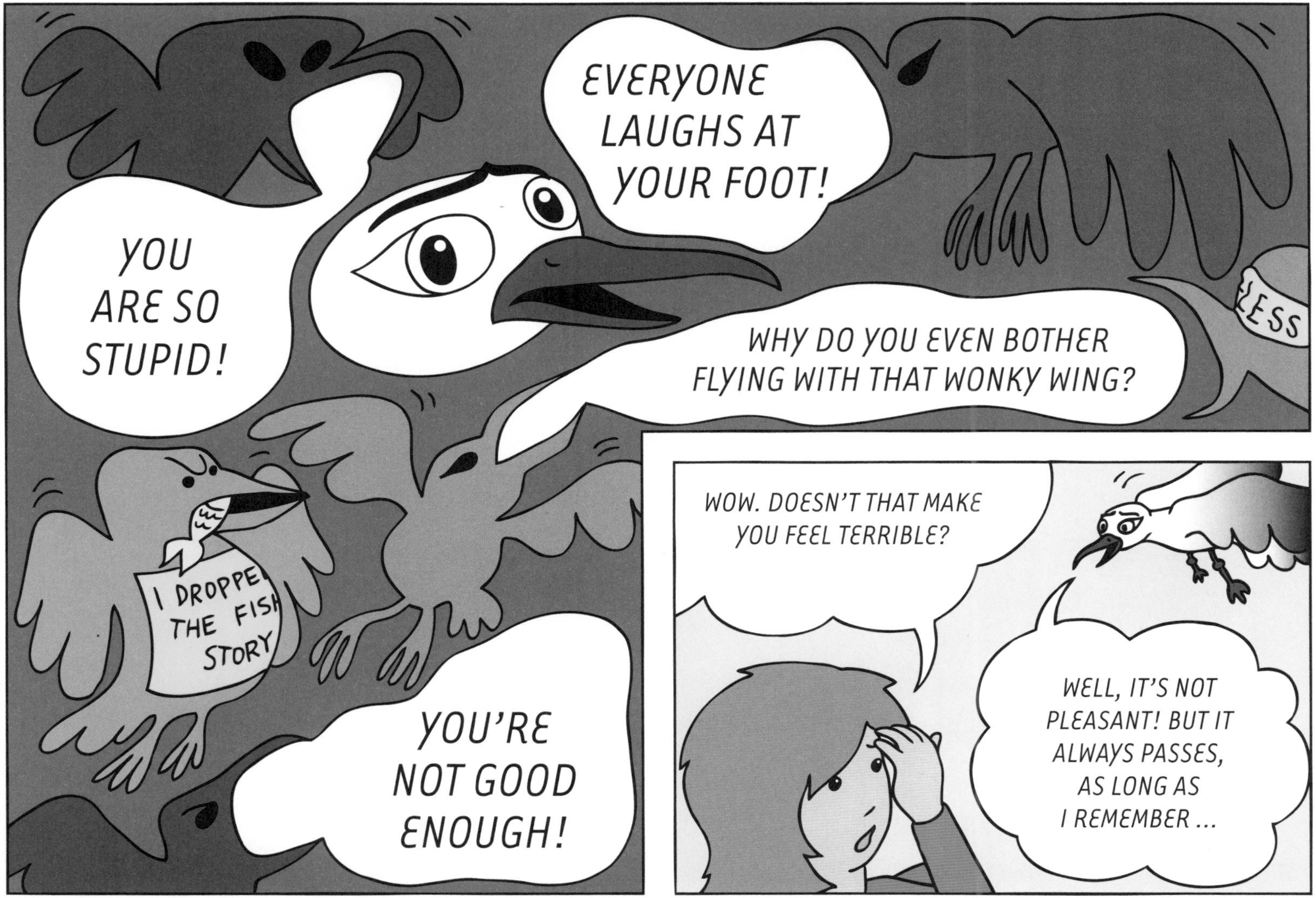
YOU ARE SO STUPID!
EVERYONE LAUGHS AT YOUR FOOT!
WHY DO YOU EVEN BOTHER FLYING WITH THAT WONKY WING?
LESS
I DROPPE THE FISH STORY
YOU'RE NOT GOOD ENOUGH!
WOW. DOESN'T THAT MAKE YOU FEEL TERRIBLE?
WELL, IT'S NOT PLEASANT! BUT IT ALWAYS PASSES, AS LONG AS I REMEMBER ...

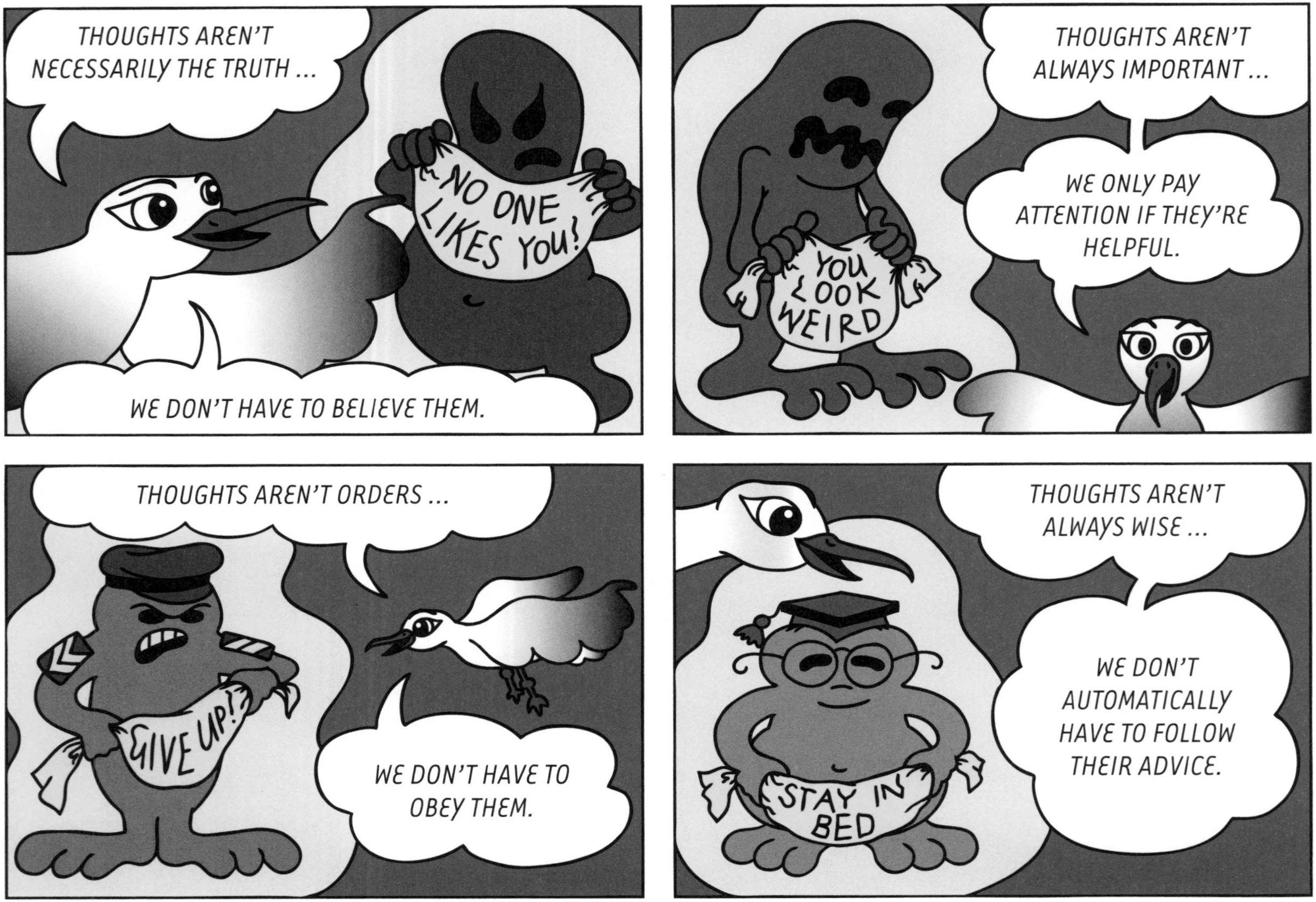
THOUGHTS AREN'T NECESSARILY THE TRUTH ...
NO ONE LIKES YOU!
WE DON'T HAVE TO BELIEVE THEM.
THOUGHTS AREN'T ALWAYS IMPORTANT ...
WE ONLY PAY ATTENTION IF THEY'RE HELPFUL.
YOU LOOK WEIRD
THOUGHTS AREN'T ORDERS ...
GIVE UP!
WE DON'T HAVE TO OBEY THEM.
THOUGHTS AREN'T ALWAYS WISE ...
WE DON'T AUTOMATICALLY HAVE TO FOLLOW THEIR ADVICE.
STAY IN BED

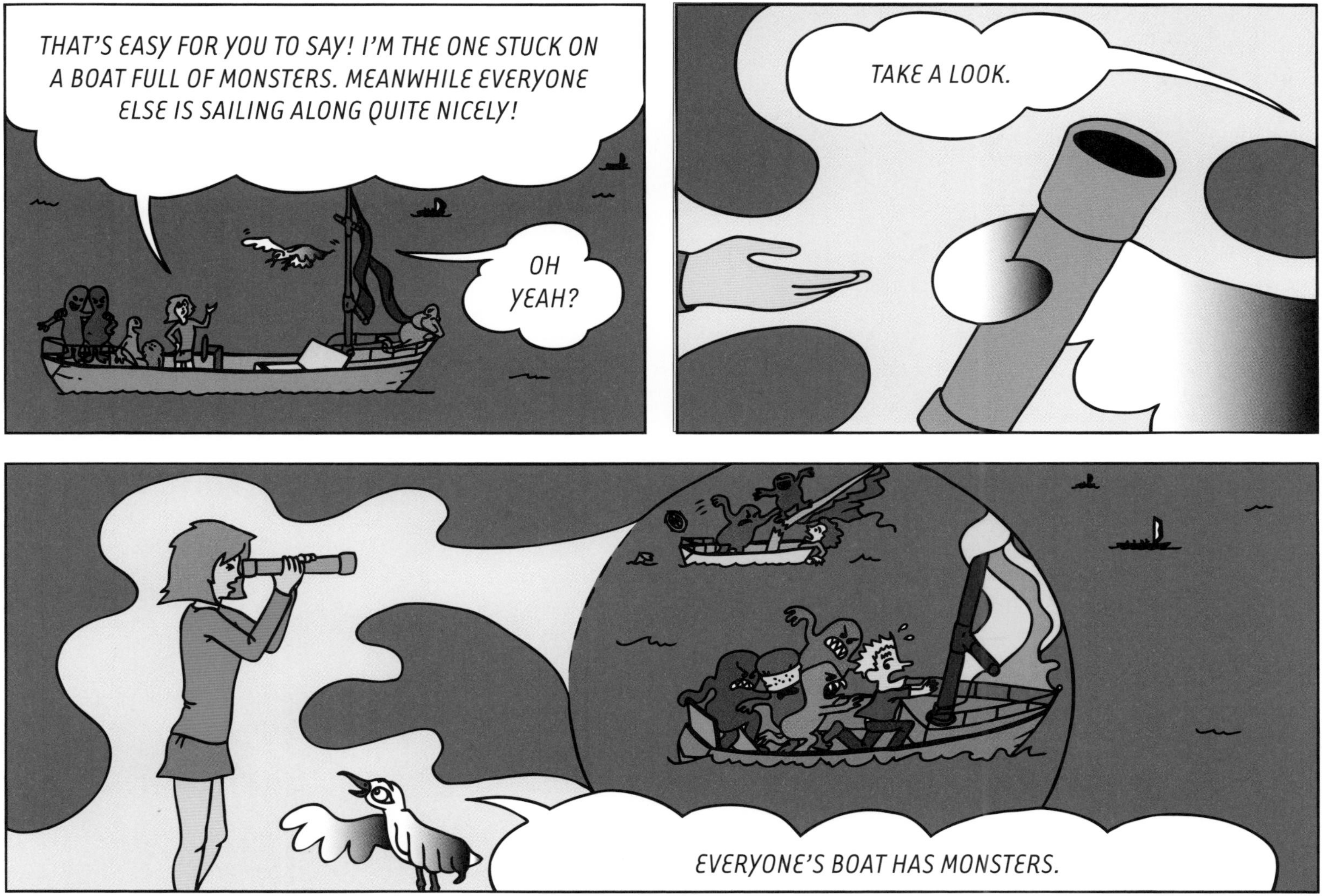
THAT'S EASY FOR YOU TO SAY! I'M THE ONE STUCK ON A BOAT FULL OF MONSTERS. MEANWHILE EVERYONE ELSE IS SAILING ALONG QUITE NICELY!
OH YEAH?
TAKE A LOOK.
EVERYONE'S BOAT HAS MONSTERS.

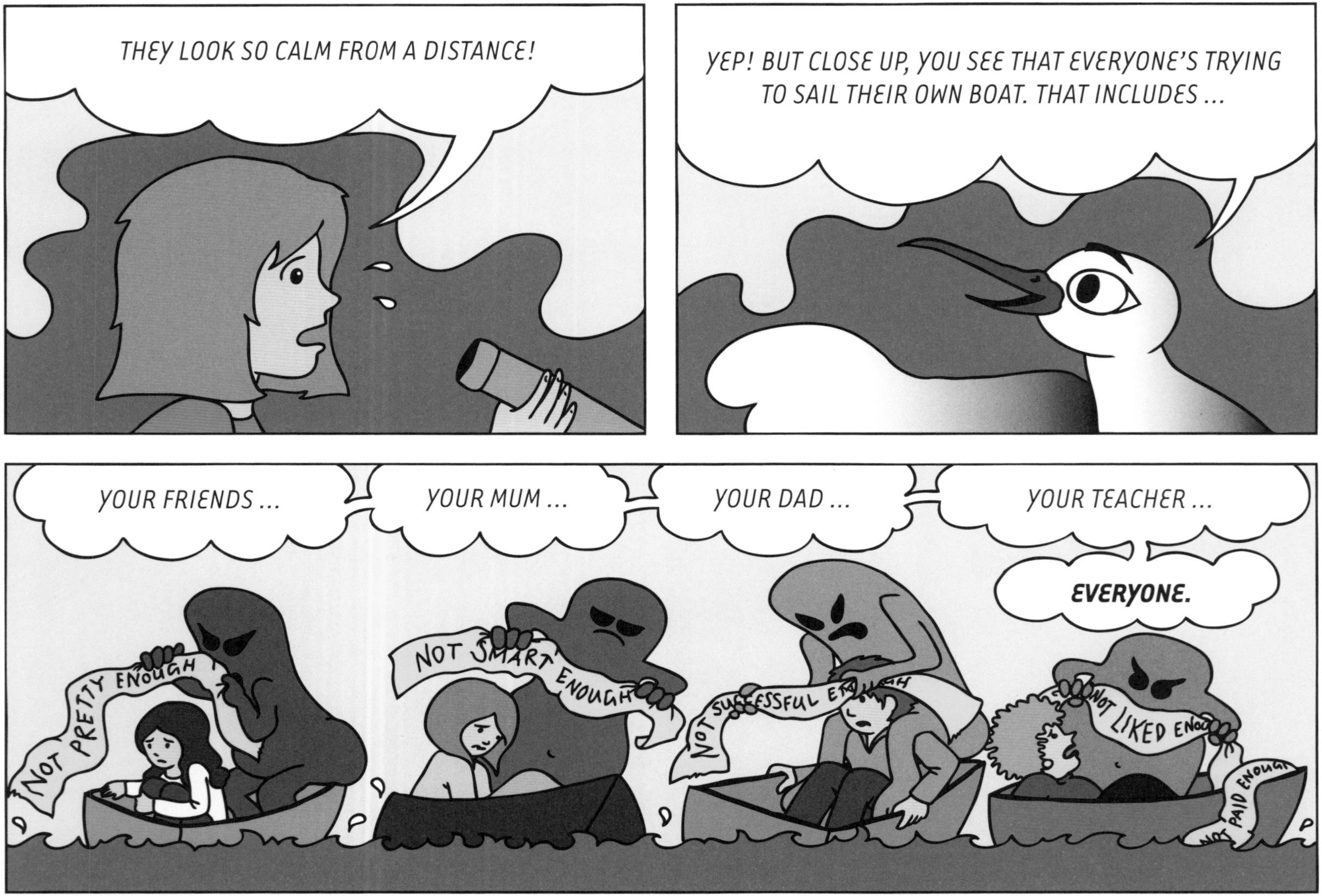
THEY LOOK SO CALM FROM A DISTANCE!
YEP! BUT CLOSE UP, YOU SEE THAT EVERYONE'S TRYING TO SAIL THEIR OWN BOAT. THAT INCLUDES ...
YOUR FRIENDS ...
YOUR MUM ...
YOUR DAD ...
YOUR TEACHER ...
EVERYONE.
NOT PRETTY ENOUGH
NOT SMART ENOUGH
NOT SUCCESSFUL
NOT LIKED
NOT PAID ENOUGH

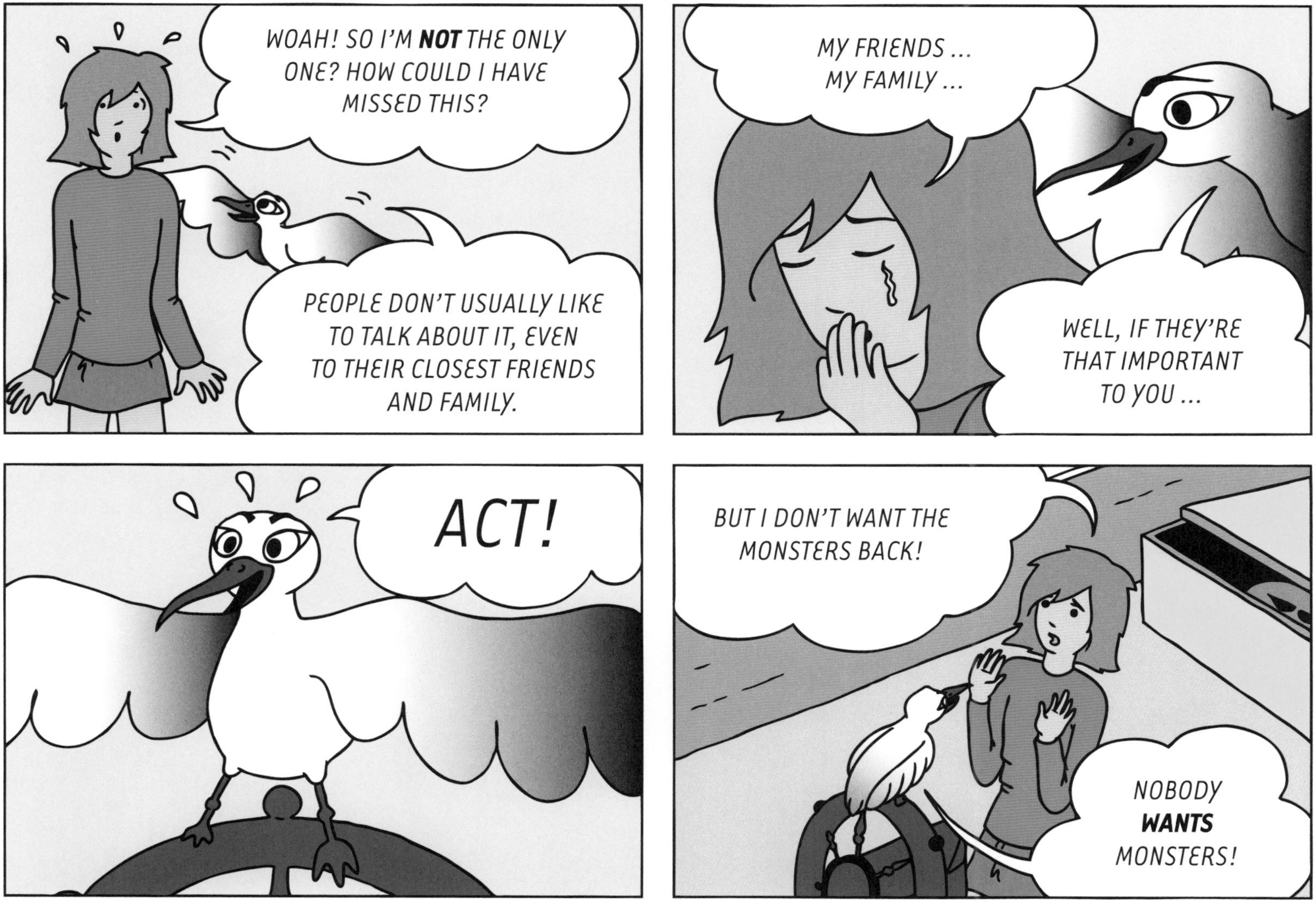
WOAH! SO I'M **NOT** THE ONLY ONE? HOW COULD I HAVE MISSED THIS?
PEOPLE DON'T USUALLY LIKE TO TALK ABOUT IT, EVEN TO THEIR CLOSEST FRIENDS AND FAMILY.
MY FRIENDS ... MY FAMILY ...
WELL, IF THEY'RE THAT IMPORTANT TO YOU ...
ACT!
BUT I DON'T WANT THE MONSTERS BACK!
NOBODY **WANTS** MONSTERS!

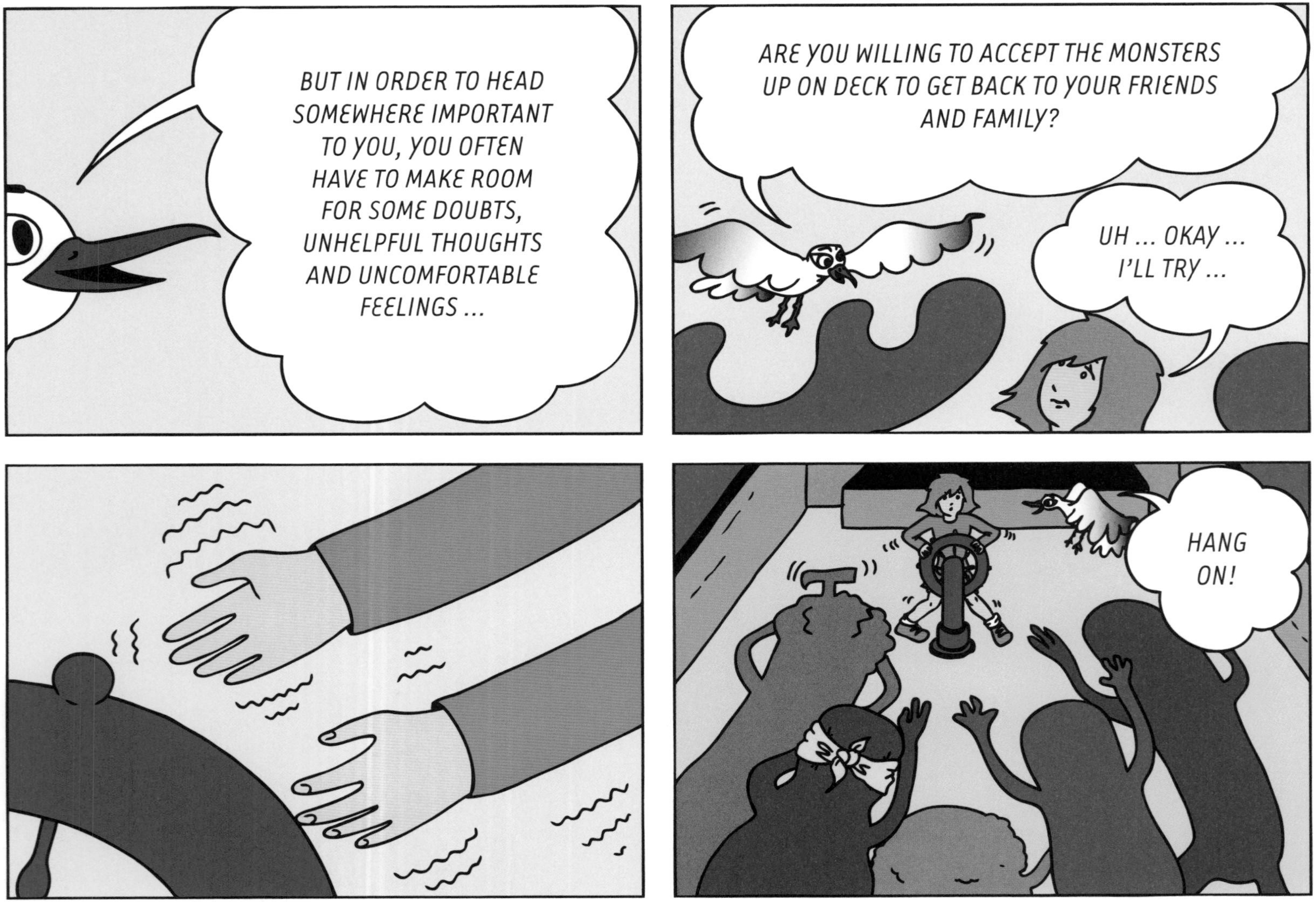
BUT IN ORDER TO HEAD SOMEWHERE IMPORTANT TO YOU, YOU OFTEN HAVE TO MAKE ROOM FOR SOME DOUBTS, UNHELPFUL THOUGHTS AND UNCOMFORTABLE FEELINGS ...
ARE YOU WILLING TO ACCEPT THE MONSTERS UP ON DECK TO GET BACK TO YOUR FRIENDS AND FAMILY?
UH ... OKAY ... I'LL TRY ...
HANG ON!

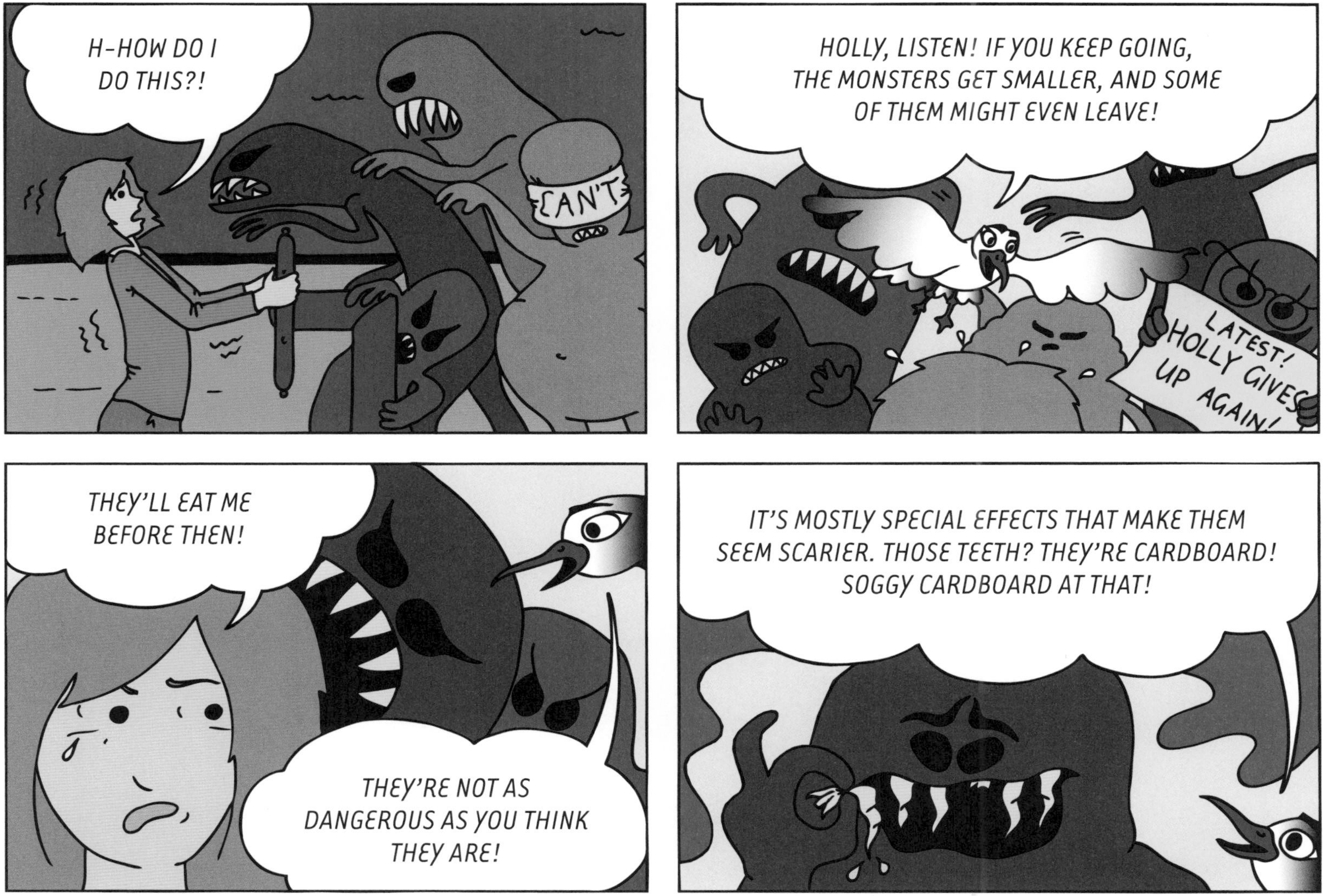
H-HOW DO I DO THIS?!
CAN'T
HOLLY, LISTEN! IF YOU KEEP GOING, THE MONSTERS GET SMALLER, AND SOME OF THEM MIGHT EVEN LEAVE!
LATEST! HOLLY GIVES UP AGAIN!
THEY'LL EAT ME BEFORE THEN!
THEY'RE NOT AS DANGEROUS AS YOU THINK THEY ARE!
IT'S MOSTLY SPECIAL EFFECTS THAT MAKE THEM SEEM SCARIER. THOSE TEETH? THEY'RE CARDBOARD! SOGGY CARDBOARD AT THAT!

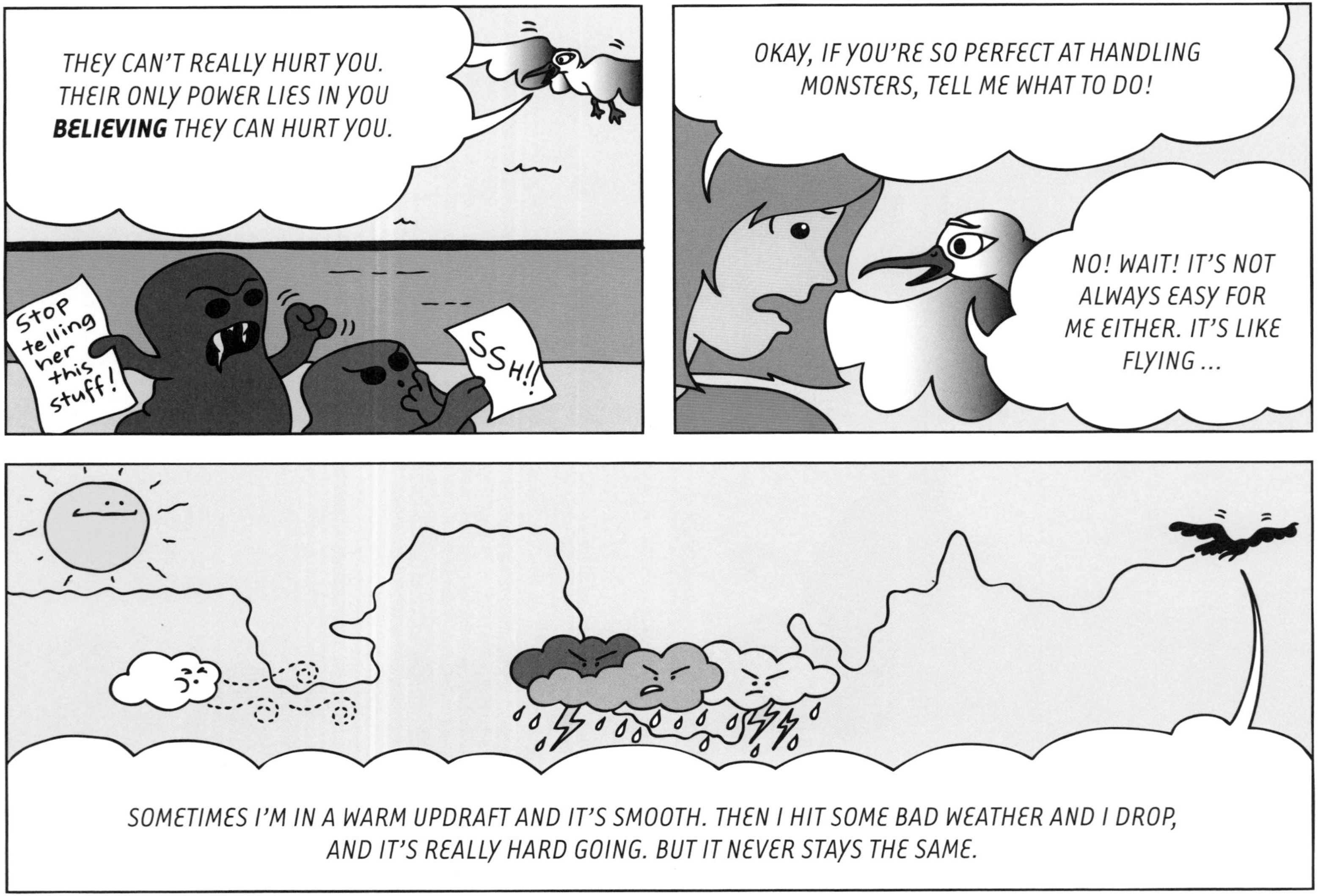
THEY CAN'T REALLY HURT YOU. THEIR ONLY POWER LIES IN YOU **BELIEVING** THEY CAN HURT YOU.
Stop telling her this stuff!
SSH!!
OKAY, IF YOU'RE SO PERFECT AT HANDLING MONSTERS, TELL ME WHAT TO DO!
NO! WAIT! IT'S NOT ALWAYS EASY FOR ME EITHER. IT'S LIKE FLYING ...
SOMETIMES I'M IN A WARM UPDRAFT AND IT'S SMOOTH. THEN I HIT SOME BAD WEATHER AND I DROP, AND IT'S REALLY HARD GOING. BUT IT NEVER STAYS THE SAME.

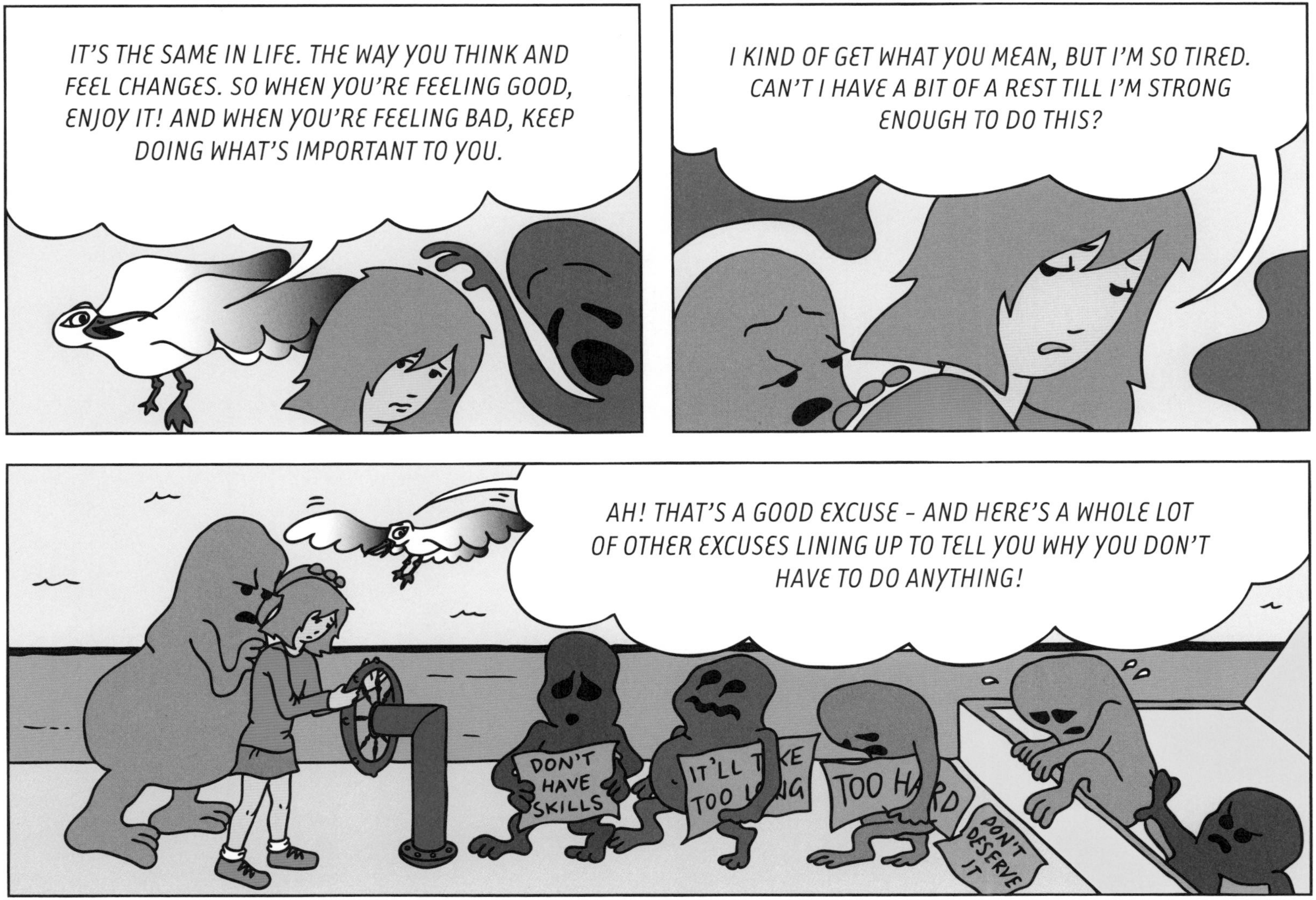
IT'S THE SAME IN LIFE. THE WAY YOU THINK AND FEEL CHANGES. SO WHEN YOU'RE FEELING GOOD, ENJOY IT! AND WHEN YOU'RE FEELING BAD, KEEP DOING WHAT'S IMPORTANT TO YOU.
I KIND OF GET WHAT YOU MEAN, BUT I'M SO TIRED. CAN'T I HAVE A BIT OF A REST TILL I'M STRONG ENOUGH TO DO THIS?
AH! THAT'S A GOOD EXCUSE – AND HERE'S A WHOLE LOT OF OTHER EXCUSES LINING UP TO TELL YOU WHY YOU DON'T HAVE TO DO ANYTHING!
DON'T HAVE SKILLS
DON'T DESERVE IT

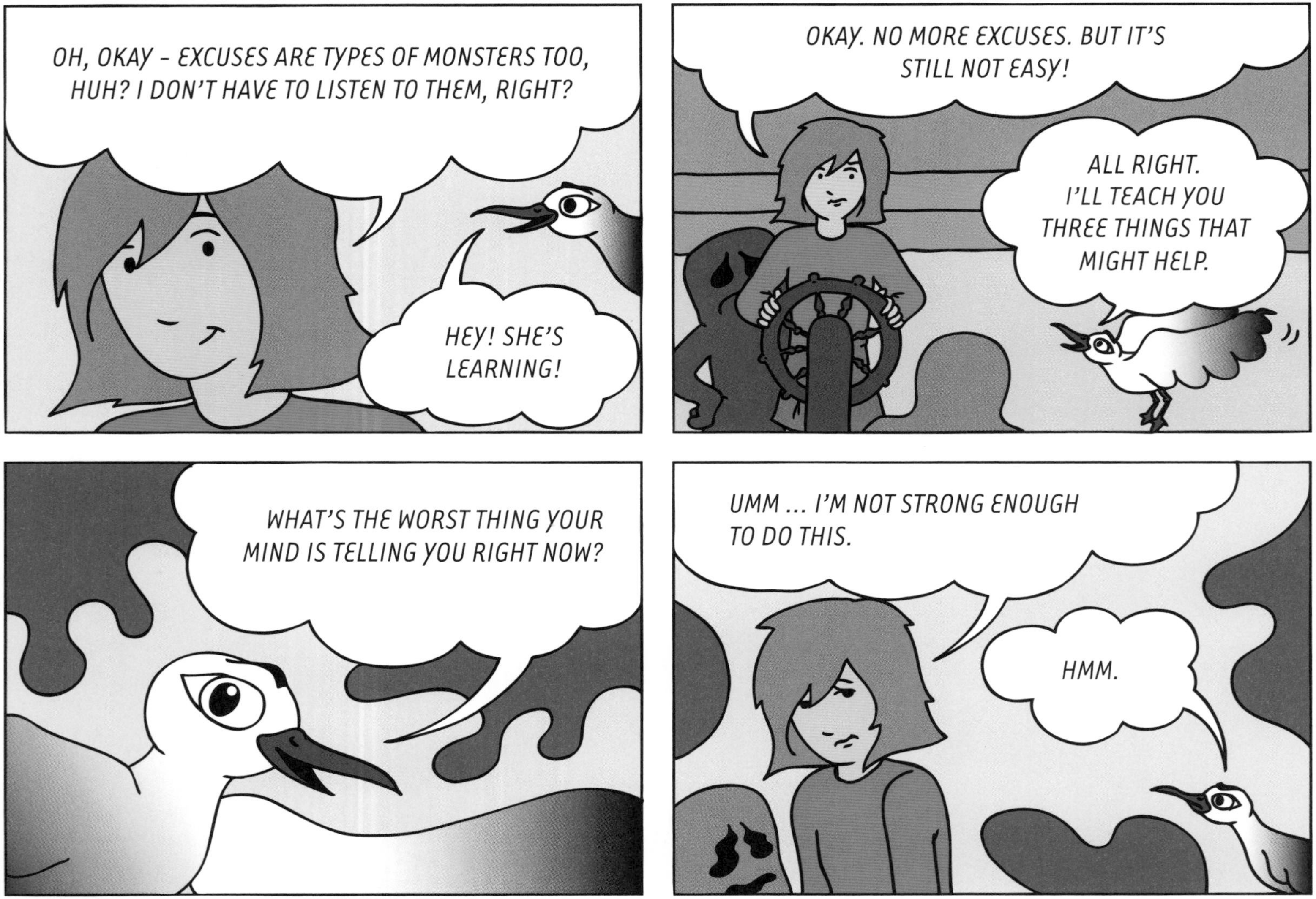
OH, OKAY – EXCUSES ARE TYPES OF MONSTERS TOO, HUH? I DON'T HAVE TO LISTEN TO THEM, RIGHT?
HEY! SHE'S LEARNING!
OKAY. NO MORE EXCUSES. BUT IT'S STILL NOT EASY!
ALL RIGHT. I'LL TEACH YOU THREE THINGS THAT MIGHT HELP.
WHAT'S THE WORST THING YOUR MIND IS TELLING YOU RIGHT NOW?
UMM ... I'M NOT STRONG ENOUGH TO DO THIS.
HMM.

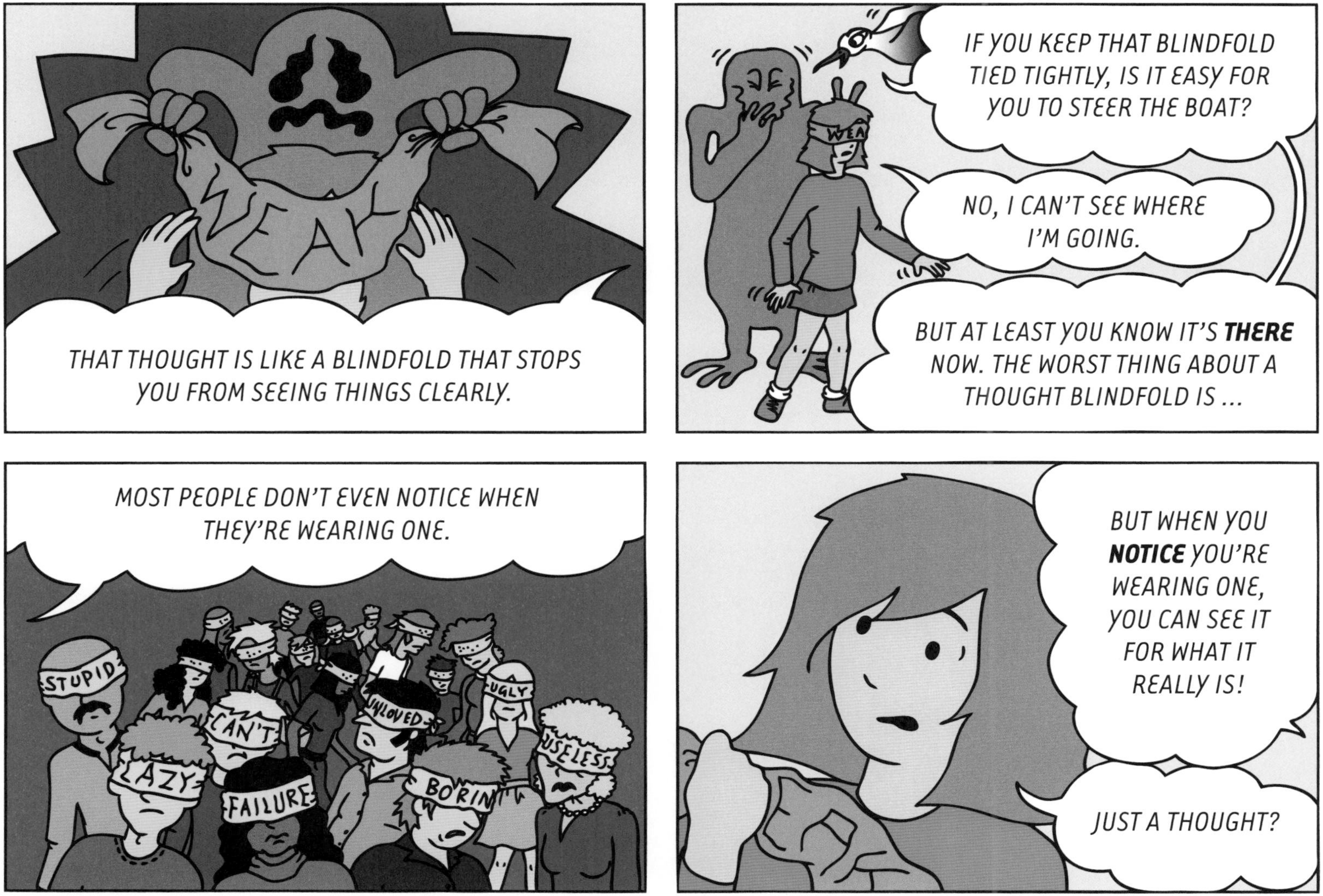
WEAK
THAT THOUGHT IS LIKE A BLINDFOLD THAT STOPS YOU FROM SEEING THINGS CLEARLY.
IF YOU KEEP THAT BLINDFOLD TIED TIGHTLY, IS IT EASY FOR YOU TO STEER THE BOAT?
WEA
NO, I CAN'T SEE WHERE I'M GOING.
BUT AT LEAST YOU KNOW IT'S **THERE** NOW. THE WORST THING ABOUT A THOUGHT BLINDFOLD IS ...
MOST PEOPLE DON'T EVEN NOTICE WHEN THEY'RE WEARING ONE.
STUPID
UGLY
UNLOVED
CAN'T
USELESS
LAZY
FAILURE
BORIN
BUT WHEN YOU **NOTICE** YOU'RE WEARING ONE, YOU CAN SEE IT FOR WHAT IT REALLY IS!
JUST A THOUGHT?

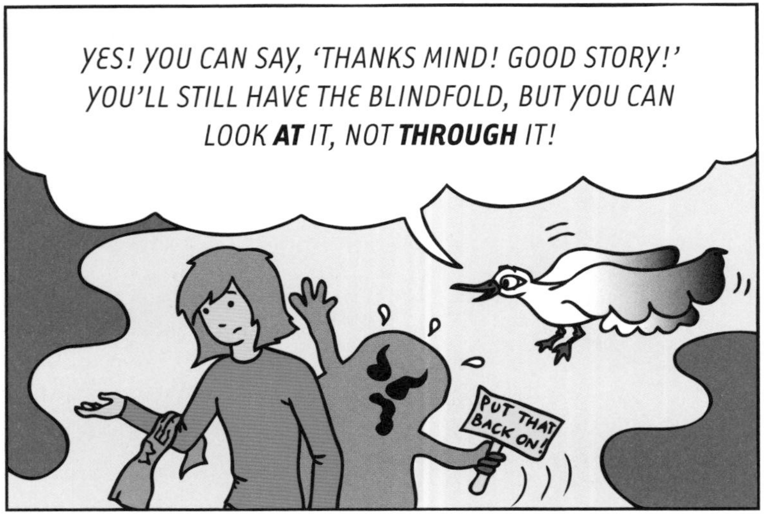
YES! YOU CAN SAY, 'THANKS MIND! GOOD STORY!' YOU'LL STILL HAVE THE BLINDFOLD, BUT YOU CAN LOOK **AT** IT, NOT **THROUGH** IT!
PUT THAT BACK ON!

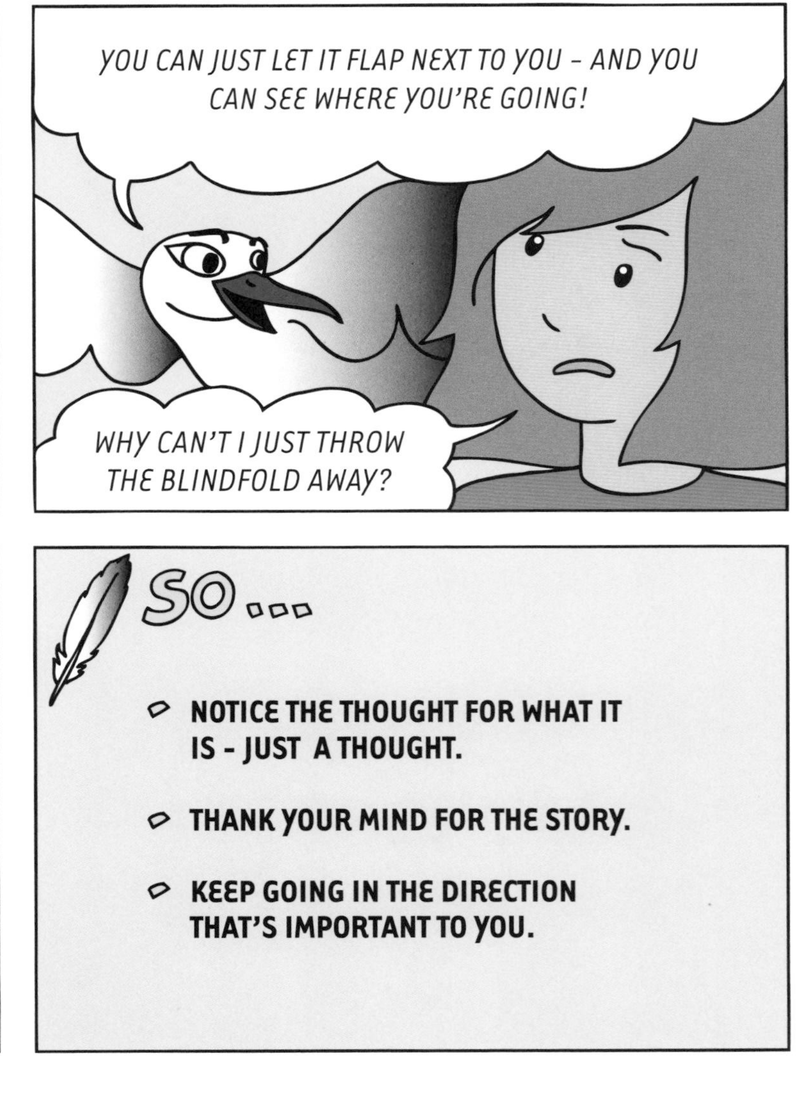
YOU CAN JUST LET IT FLAP NEXT TO YOU – AND YOU CAN SEE WHERE YOU'RE GOING!
WHY CAN'T I JUST THROW THE BLINDFOLD AWAY?

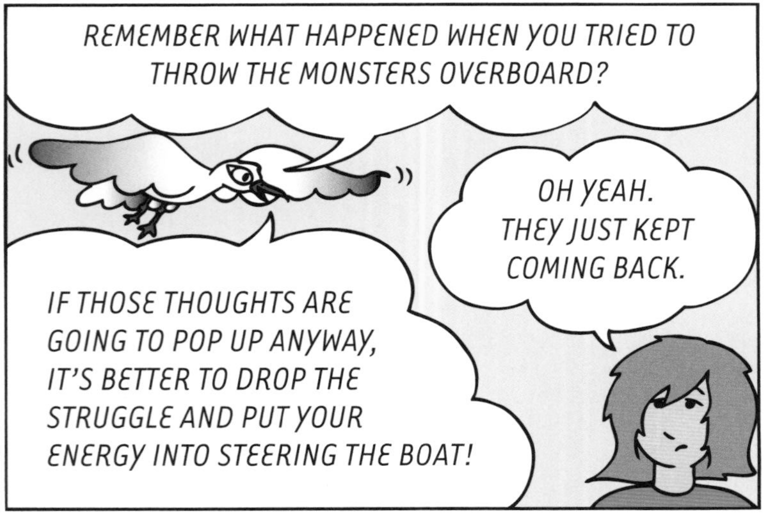
REMEMBER WHAT HAPPENED WHEN YOU TRIED TO THROW THE MONSTERS OVERBOARD?
OH YEAH. THEY JUST KEPT COMING BACK.
IF THOSE THOUGHTS ARE GOING TO POP UP ANYWAY, IT'S BETTER TO DROP THE STRUGGLE AND PUT YOUR ENERGY INTO STEERING THE BOAT!

SO...

- **NOTICE THE THOUGHT FOR WHAT IT IS - JUST A THOUGHT.**
- **THANK YOUR MIND FOR THE STORY.**
- **KEEP GOING IN THE DIRECTION THAT'S IMPORTANT TO YOU.**

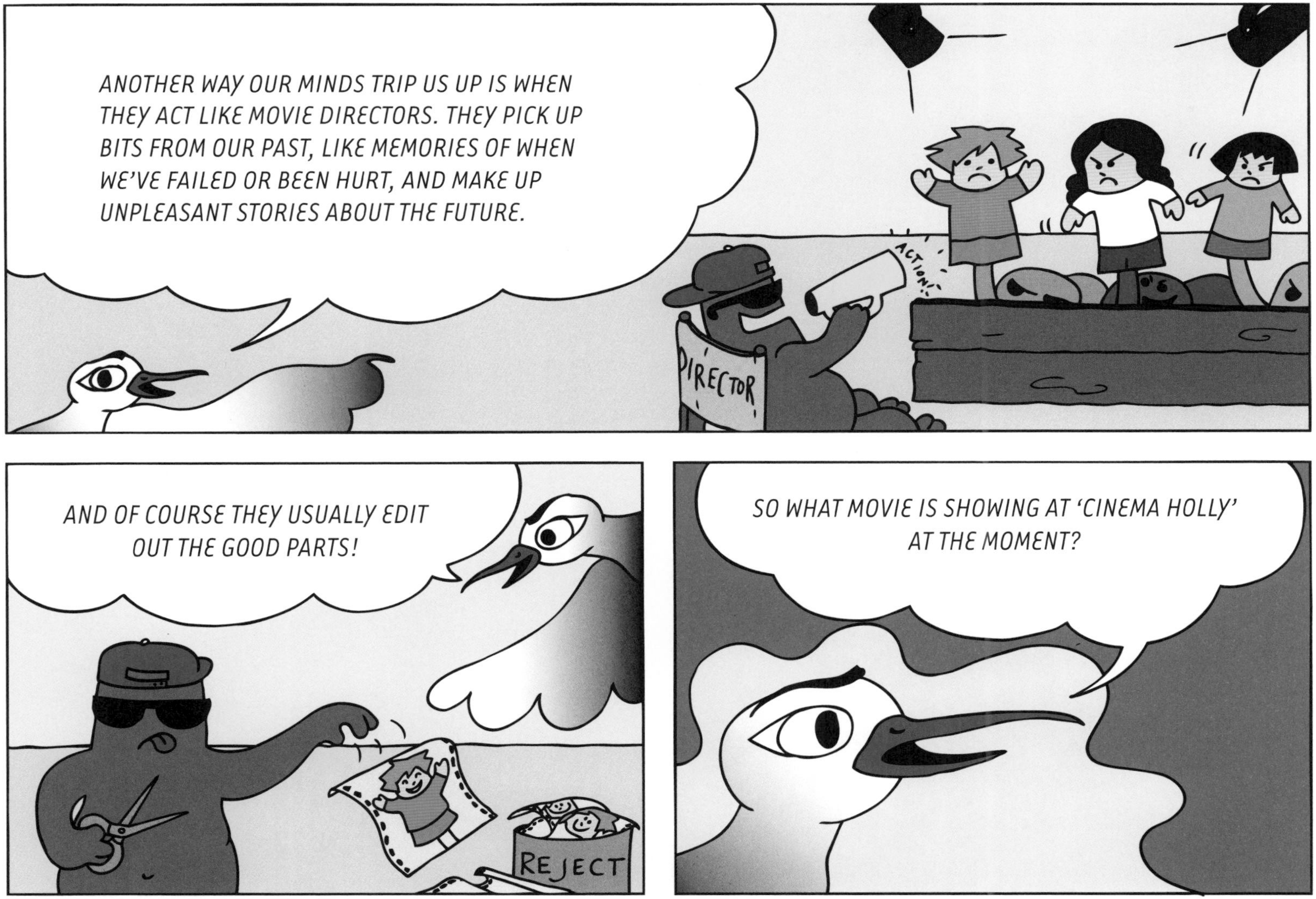
ANOTHER WAY OUR MINDS TRIP US UP IS WHEN THEY ACT LIKE MOVIE DIRECTORS. THEY PICK UP BITS FROM OUR PAST, LIKE MEMORIES OF WHEN WE'VE FAILED OR BEEN HURT, AND MAKE UP UNPLEASANT STORIES ABOUT THE FUTURE.
ACTION!
DIRECTOR
AND OF COURSE THEY USUALLY EDIT OUT THE GOOD PARTS!
REJECT
SO WHAT MOVIE IS SHOWING AT 'CINEMA HOLLY' AT THE MOMENT?

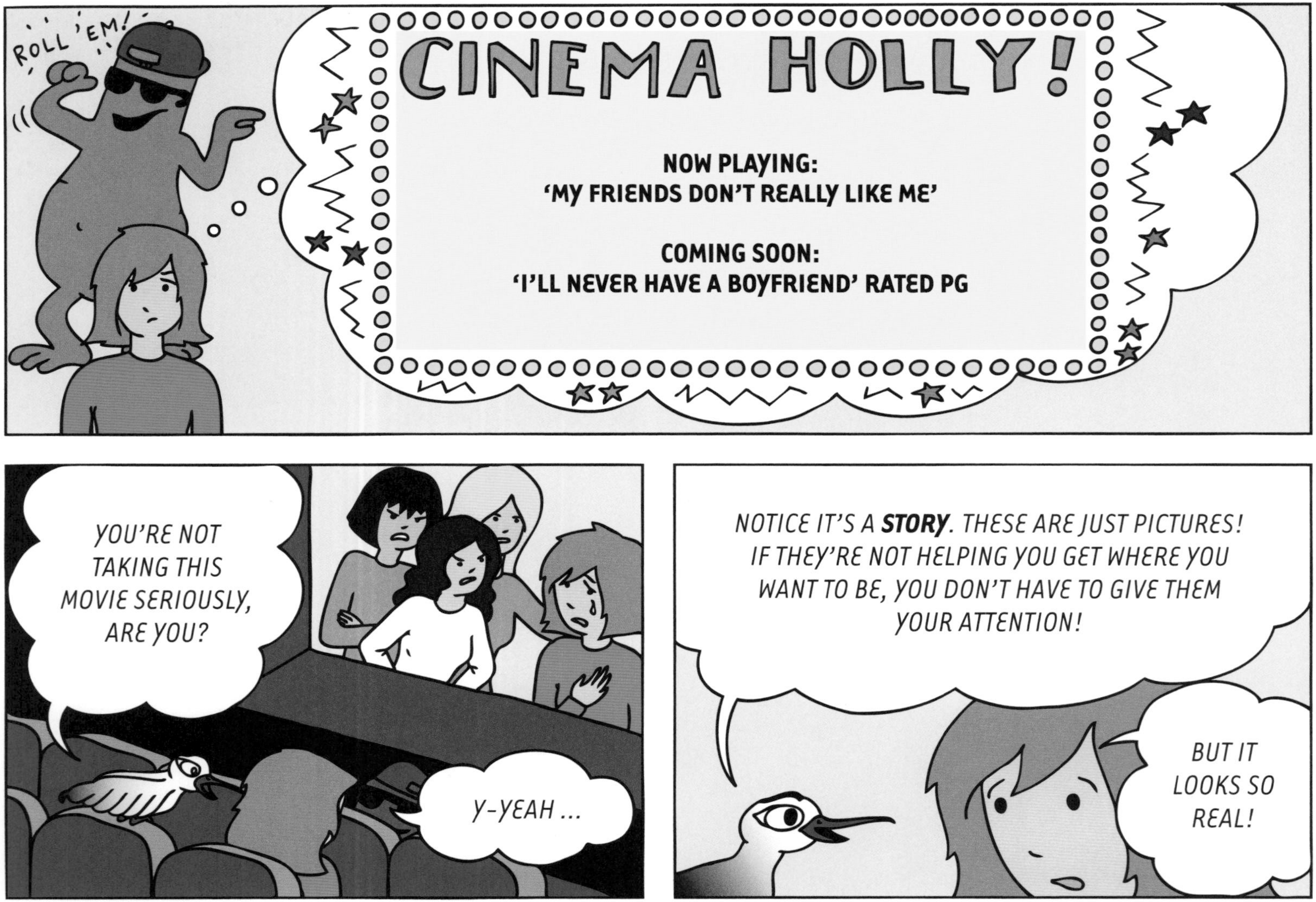
ROLL 'EM!
CINEMA HOLLY!
NOW PLAYING:
'MY FRIENDS DON'T REALLY LIKE ME'
COMING SOON:
'I'LL NEVER HAVE A BOYFRIEND' RATED PG
YOU'RE NOT TAKING THIS MOVIE SERIOUSLY, ARE YOU?
Y-YEAH ...
NOTICE IT'S A STORY. THESE ARE JUST PICTURES! IF THEY'RE NOT HELPING YOU GET WHERE YOU WANT TO BE, YOU DON'T HAVE TO GIVE THEM YOUR ATTENTION!
BUT IT LOOKS SO REAL!

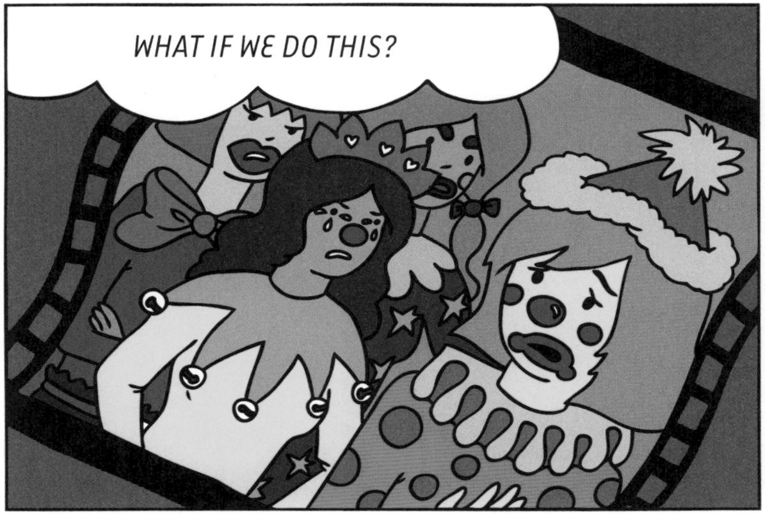
WHAT IF WE DO THIS?

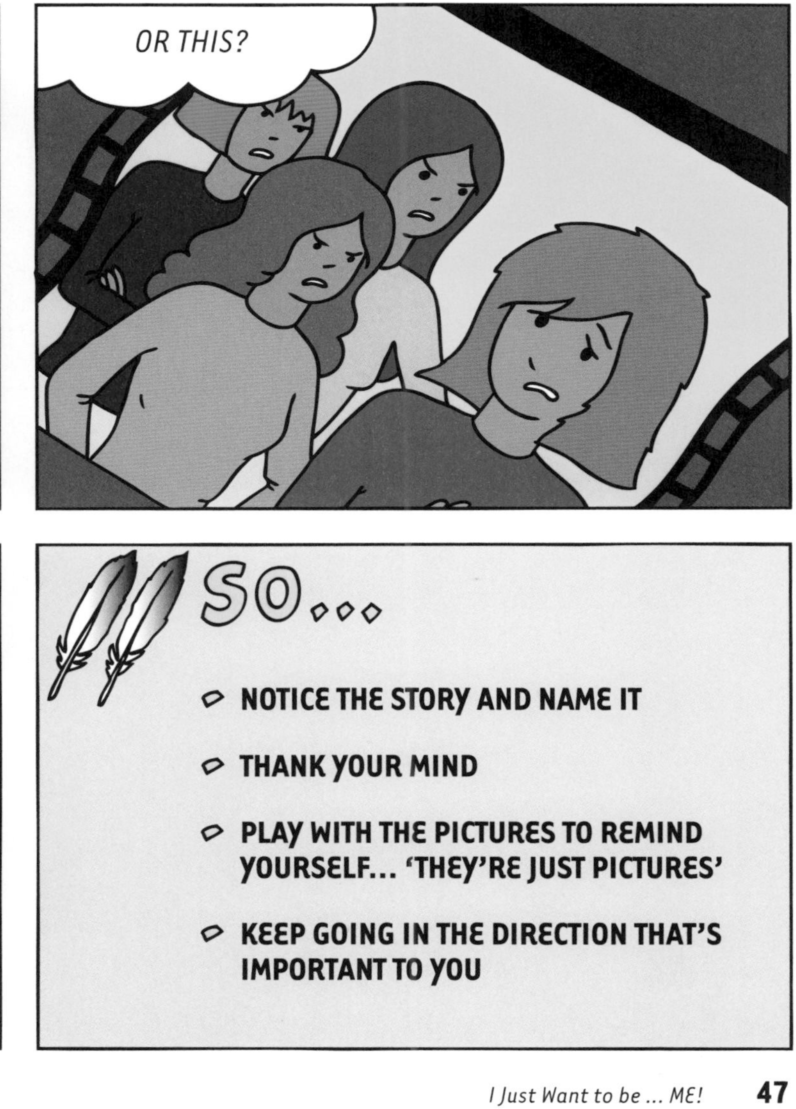
OR THIS?

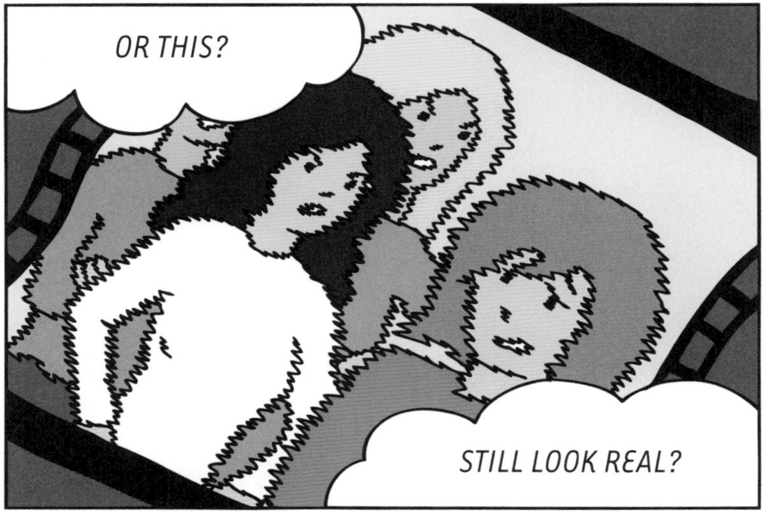
OR THIS?
STILL LOOK REAL?

SO...

- NOTICE THE STORY AND NAME IT
- THANK YOUR MIND
- PLAY WITH THE PICTURES TO REMIND YOURSELF... 'THEY'RE JUST PICTURES'
- KEEP GOING IN THE DIRECTION THAT'S IMPORTANT TO YOU

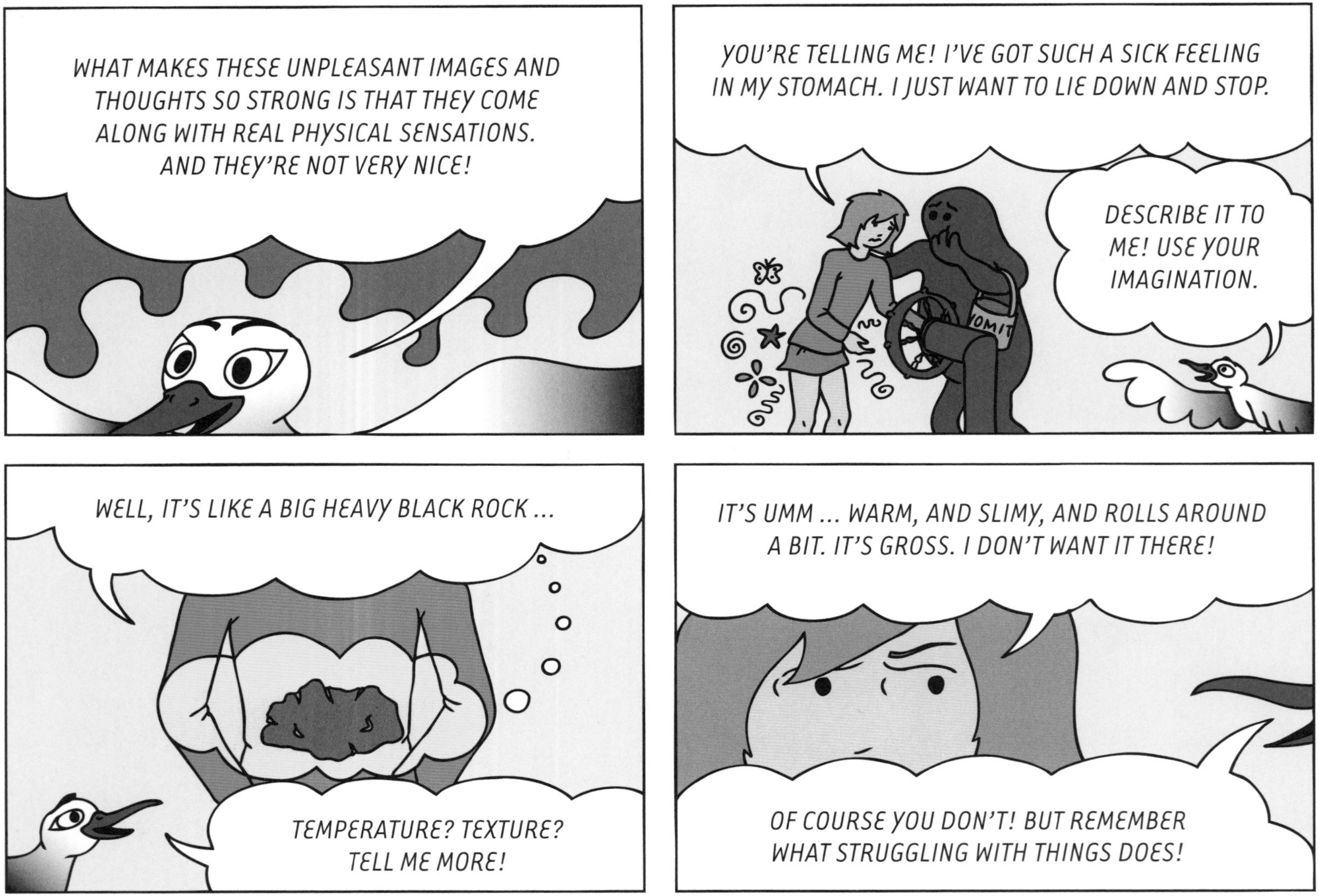
WHAT MAKES THESE UNPLEASANT IMAGES AND THOUGHTS SO STRONG IS THAT THEY COME ALONG WITH REAL PHYSICAL SENSATIONS. AND THEY'RE NOT VERY NICE!
YOU'RE TELLING ME! I'VE GOT SUCH A SICK FEELING IN MY STOMACH. I JUST WANT TO LIE DOWN AND STOP.
DESCRIBE IT TO ME! USE YOUR IMAGINATION.
WELL, IT'S LIKE A BIG HEAVY BLACK ROCK ...
TEMPERATURE? TEXTURE? TELL ME MORE!
IT'S UMM ... WARM, AND SLIMY, AND ROLLS AROUND A BIT. IT'S GROSS. I DON'T WANT IT THERE!
OF COURSE YOU DON'T! BUT REMEMBER WHAT STRUGGLING WITH THINGS DOES!

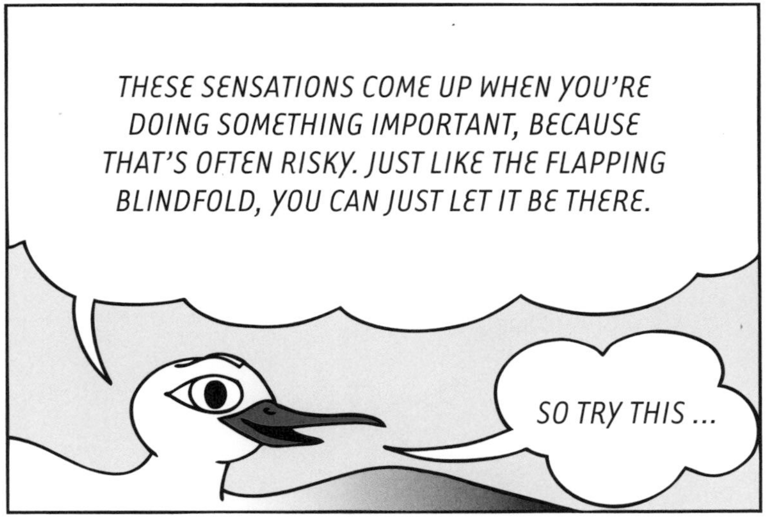
THESE SENSATIONS COME UP WHEN YOU'RE DOING SOMETHING IMPORTANT, BECAUSE THAT'S OFTEN RISKY. JUST LIKE THE FLAPPING BLINDFOLD, YOU CAN JUST LET IT BE THERE.
SO TRY THIS ...

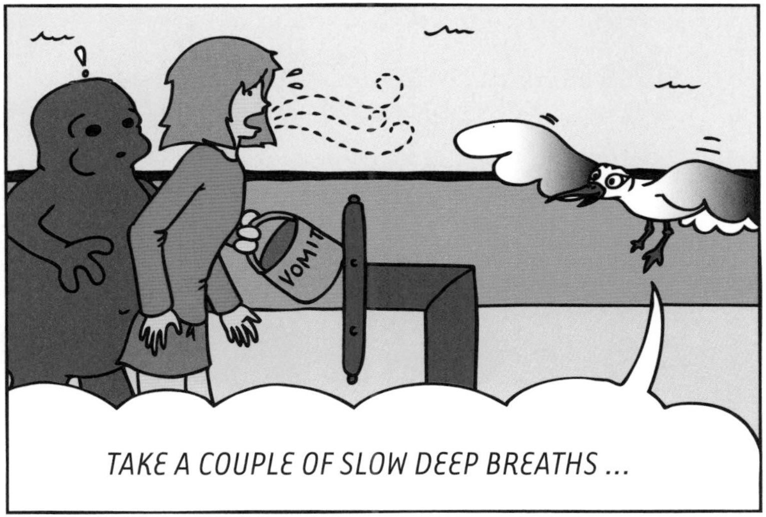
VOMIT
TAKE A COUPLE OF SLOW DEEP BREATHS ...

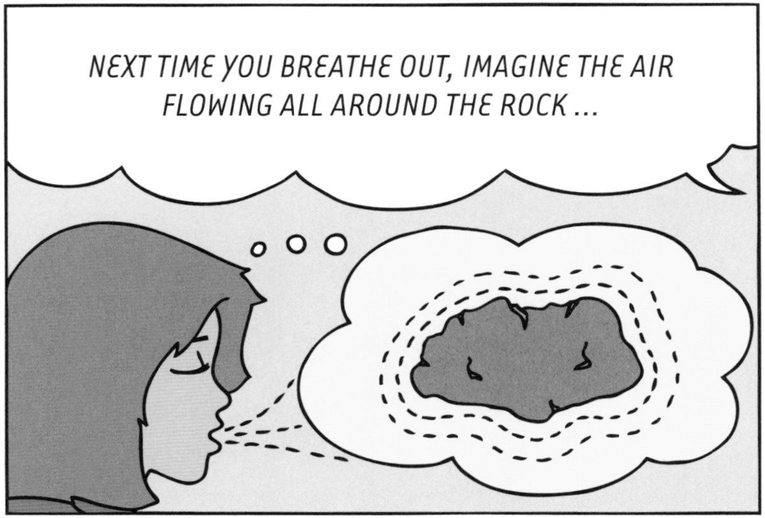
NEXT TIME YOU BREATHE OUT, IMAGINE THE AIR FLOWING ALL AROUND THE ROCK ...

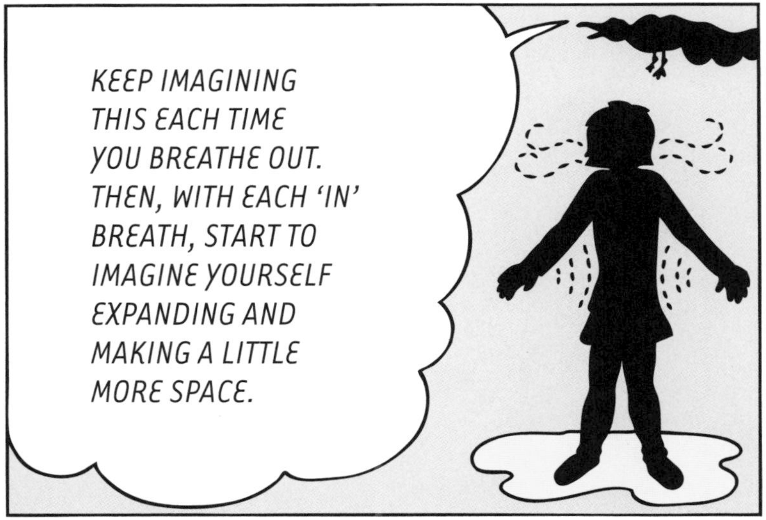
KEEP IMAGINING THIS EACH TIME YOU BREATHE OUT. THEN, WITH EACH 'IN' BREATH, START TO IMAGINE YOURSELF EXPANDING AND MAKING A LITTLE MORE SPACE.

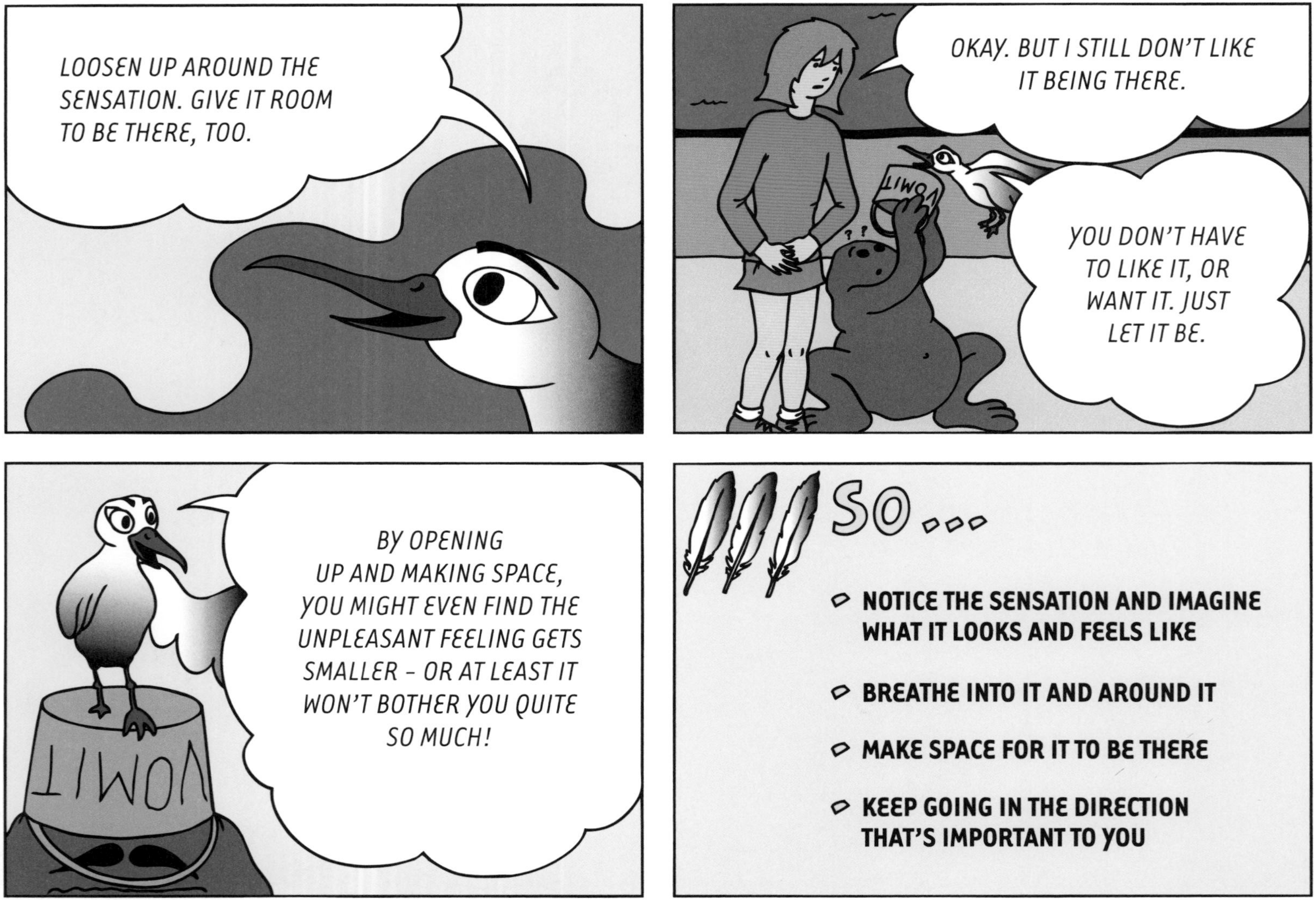
LOOSEN UP AROUND THE SENSATION. GIVE IT ROOM TO BE THERE, TOO.
OKAY. BUT I STILL DON'T LIKE IT BEING THERE.
YOU DON'T HAVE TO LIKE IT, OR WANT IT. JUST LET IT BE.
BY OPENING UP AND MAKING SPACE, YOU MIGHT EVEN FIND THE UNPLEASANT FEELING GETS SMALLER – OR AT LEAST IT WON'T BOTHER YOU QUITE SO MUCH!
SO ...
NOTICE THE SENSATION AND IMAGINE WHAT IT LOOKS AND FEELS LIKE
BREATHE INTO IT AND AROUND IT
MAKE SPACE FOR IT TO BE THERE
KEEP GOING IN THE DIRECTION THAT'S IMPORTANT TO YOU

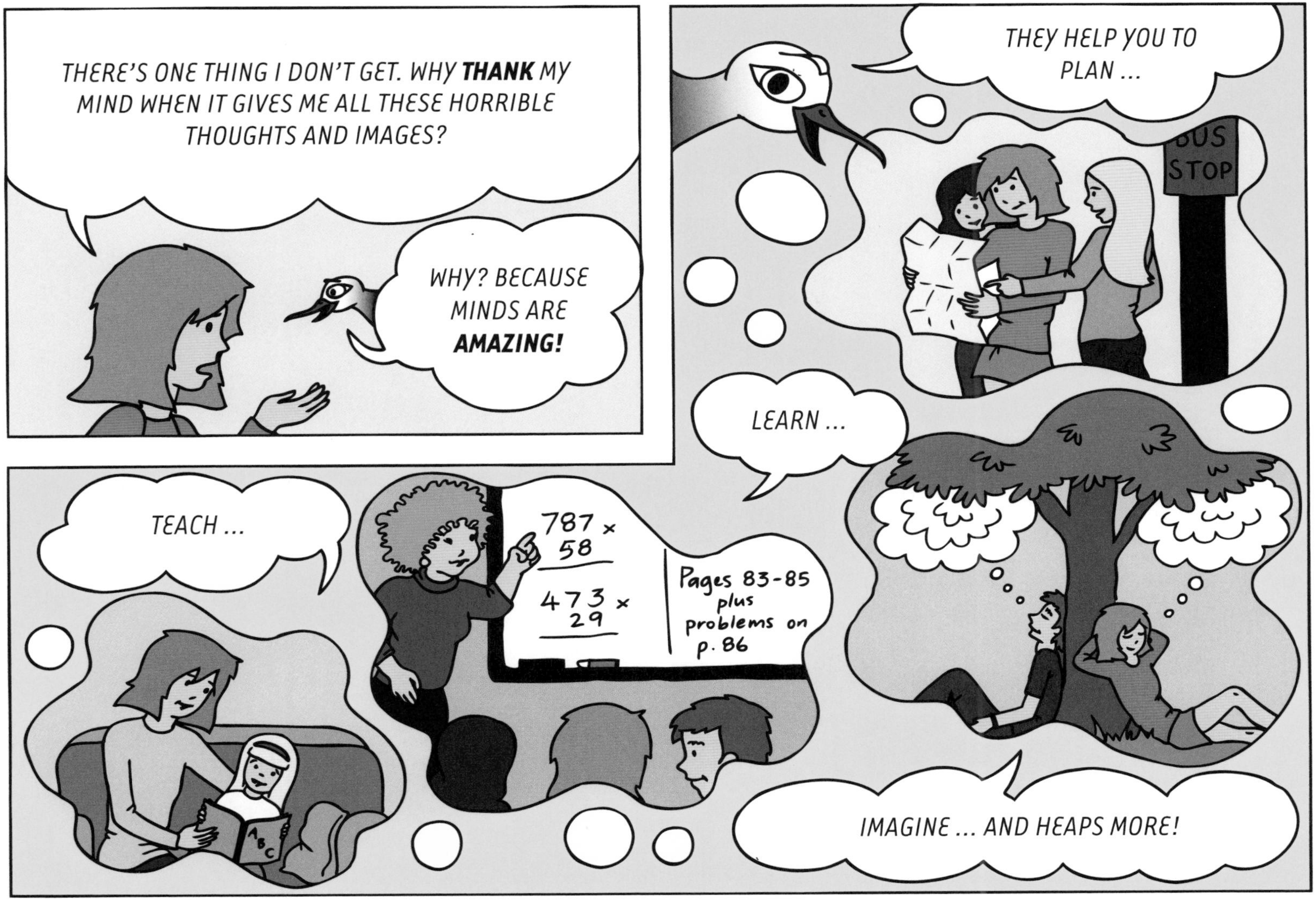
THERE'S ONE THING I DON'T GET. WHY **THANK** MY MIND WHEN IT GIVES ME ALL THESE HORRIBLE THOUGHTS AND IMAGES?
WHY? BECAUSE MINDS ARE **AMAZING!**
THEY HELP YOU TO PLAN ...
BUS STOP
LEARN ...
TEACH ...
787 × 58
473 × 29
Pages 83-85 plus problems on p. 86
ABC
IMAGINE ... AND HEAPS MORE!

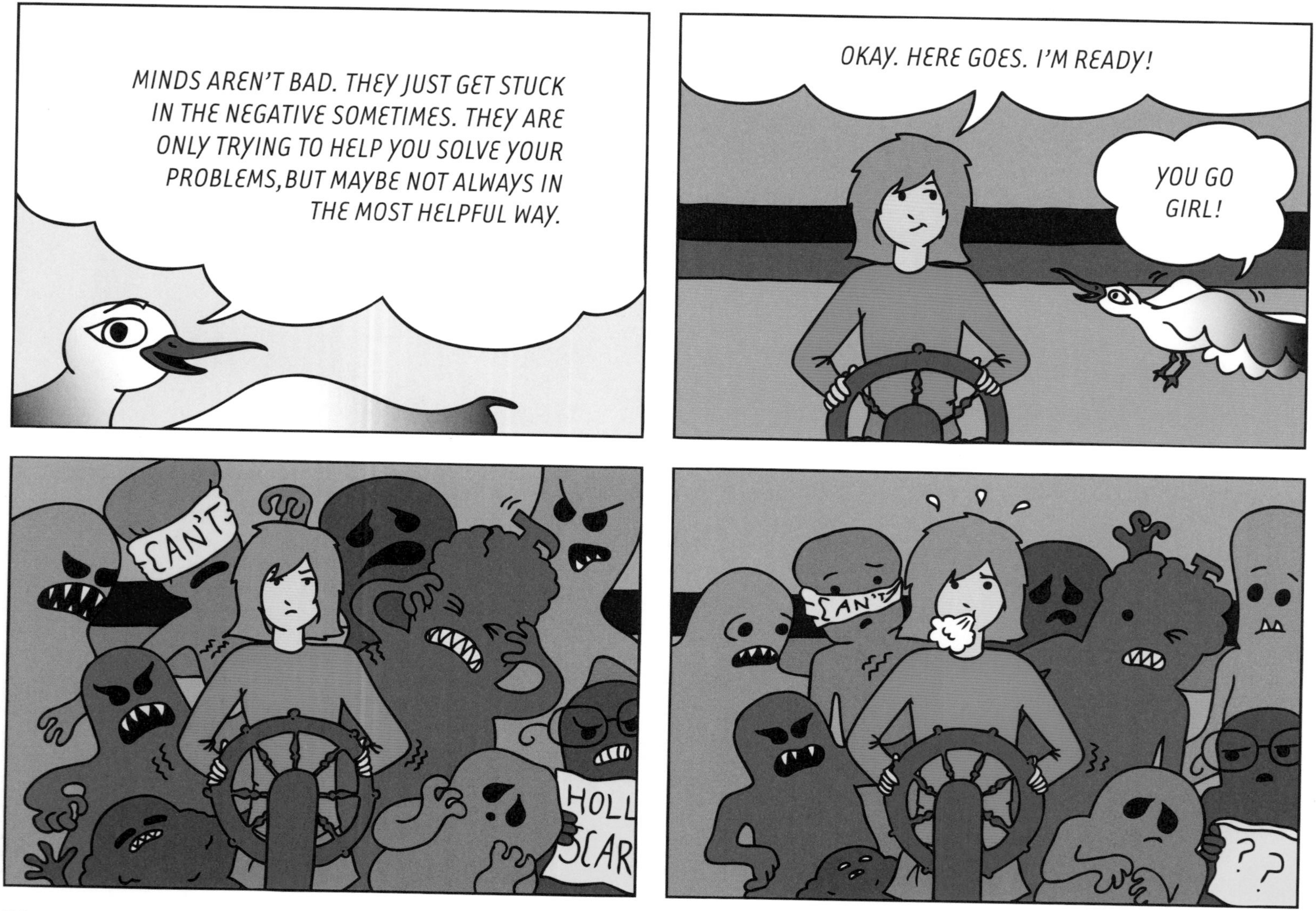
MINDS AREN'T BAD. THEY JUST GET STUCK IN THE NEGATIVE SOMETIMES. THEY ARE ONLY TRYING TO HELP YOU SOLVE YOUR PROBLEMS, BUT MAYBE NOT ALWAYS IN THE MOST HELPFUL WAY.
OKAY. HERE GOES. I'M READY!
YOU GO GIRL!
CAN'T
HOLL
SCAR
CAN'T
??

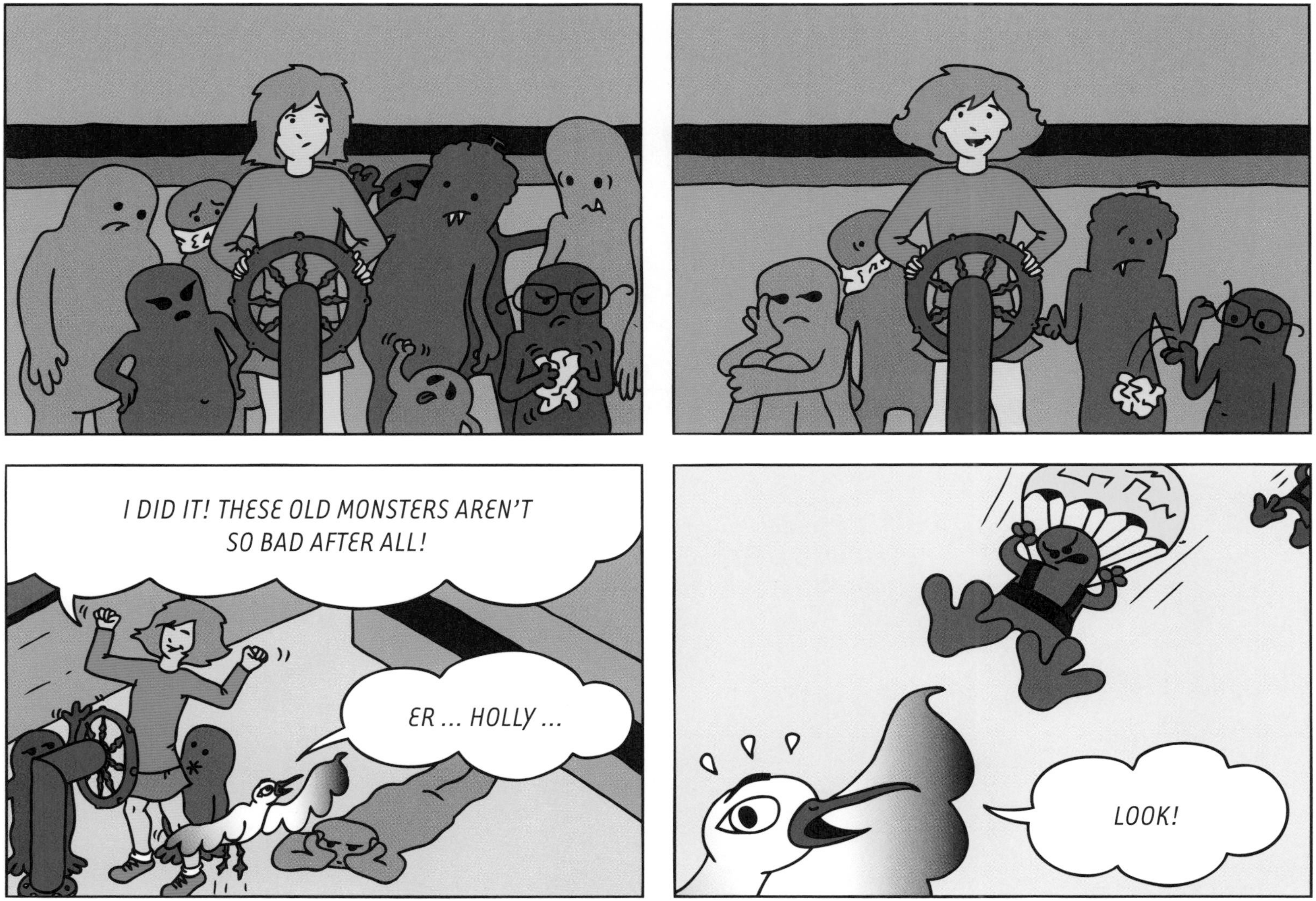
I DID IT! THESE OLD MONSTERS AREN'T SO BAD AFTER ALL!
ER ... HOLLY ...
LOOK!

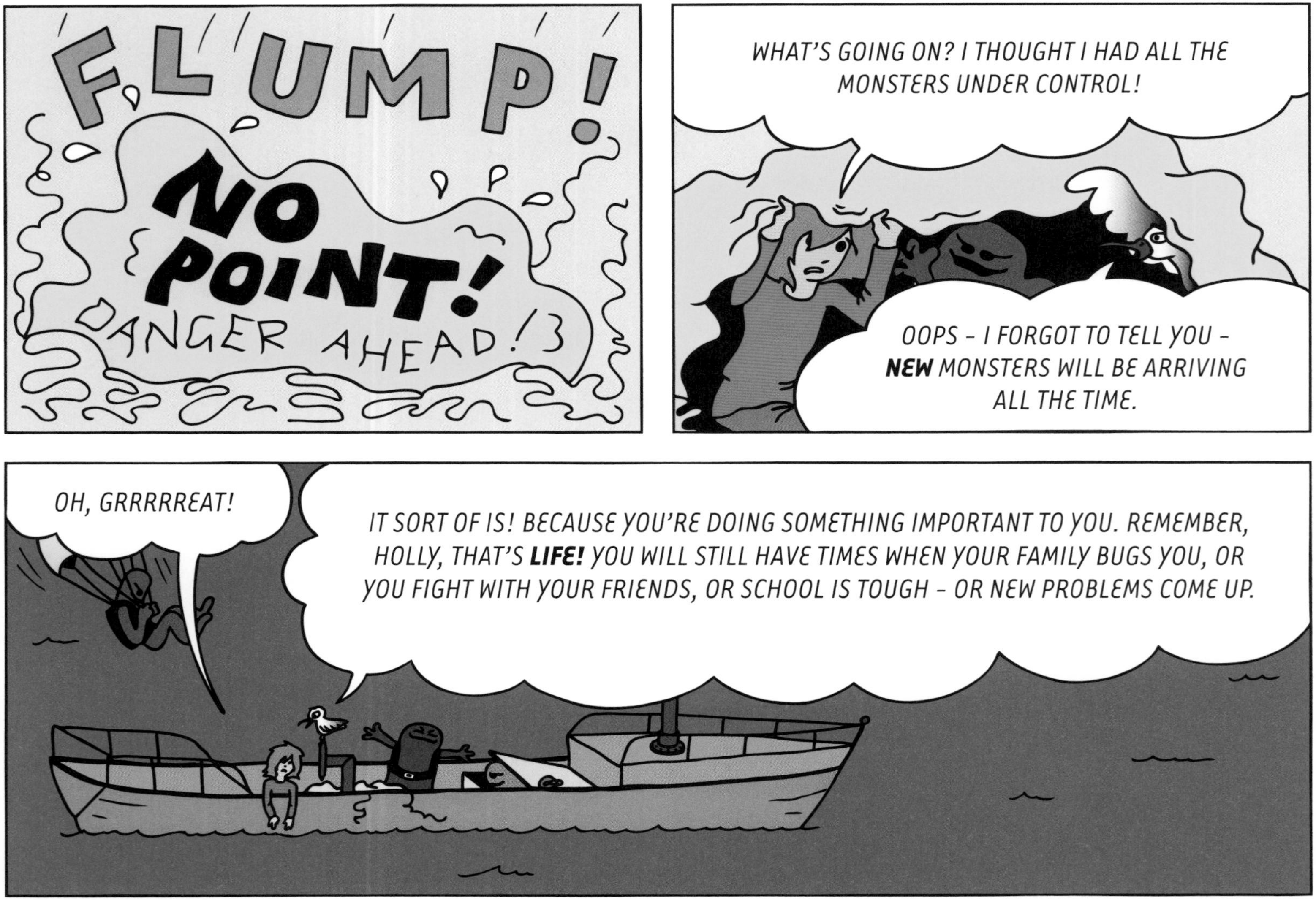
FLUMP!
NO POINT!
DANGER AHEAD!
WHAT'S GOING ON? I THOUGHT I HAD ALL THE MONSTERS UNDER CONTROL!
OOPS - I FORGOT TO TELL YOU - NEW MONSTERS WILL BE ARRIVING ALL THE TIME.
OH, GRRRRREAT!
IT SORT OF IS! BECAUSE YOU'RE DOING SOMETHING IMPORTANT TO YOU. REMEMBER, HOLLY, THAT'S LIFE! YOU WILL STILL HAVE TIMES WHEN YOUR FAMILY BUGS YOU, OR YOU FIGHT WITH YOUR FRIENDS, OR SCHOOL IS TOUGH - OR NEW PROBLEMS COME UP.

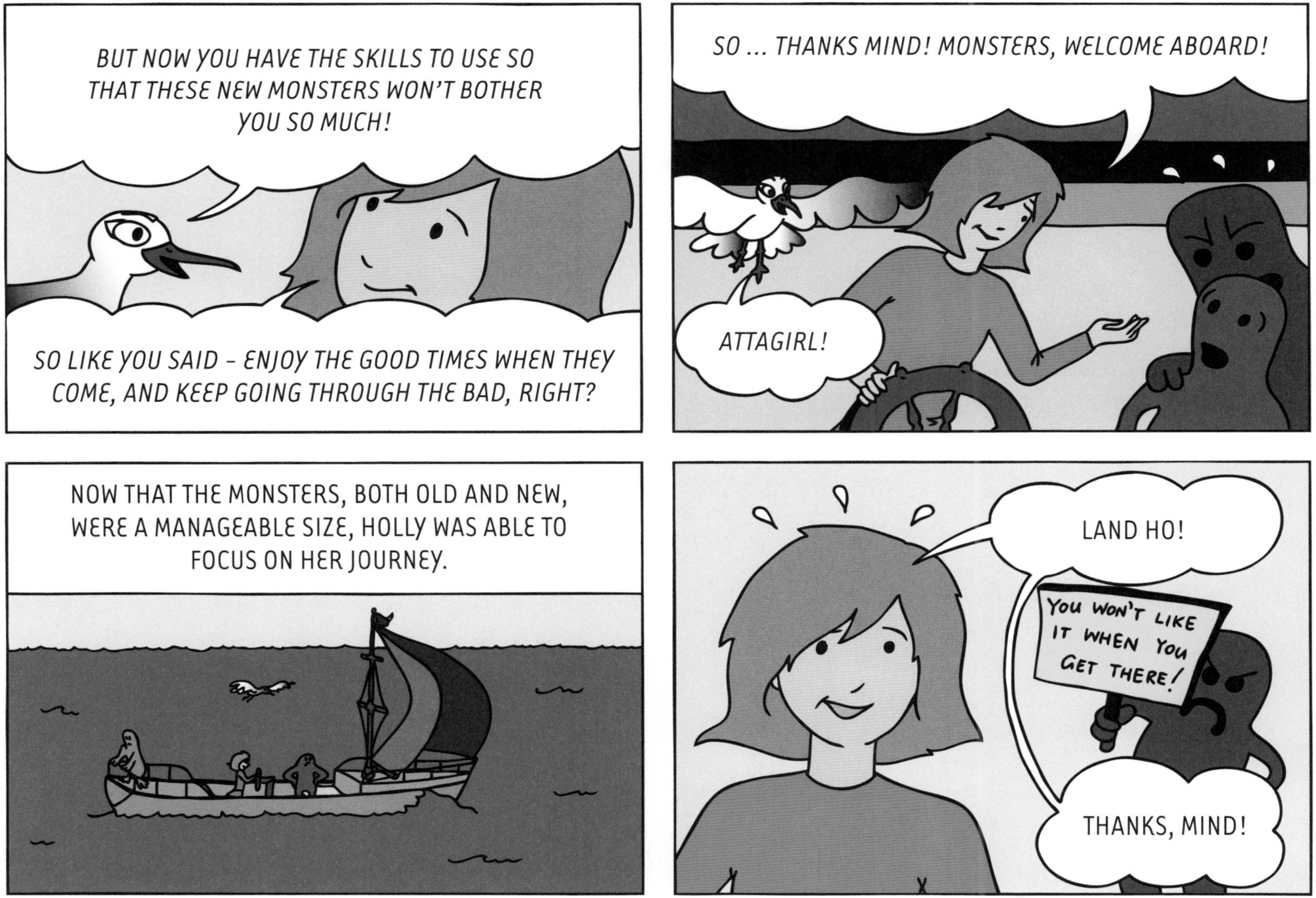
BUT NOW YOU HAVE THE SKILLS TO USE SO THAT THESE NEW MONSTERS WON'T BOTHER YOU SO MUCH!
SO LIKE YOU SAID – ENJOY THE GOOD TIMES WHEN THEY COME, AND KEEP GOING THROUGH THE BAD, RIGHT?
SO ... THANKS MIND! MONSTERS, WELCOME ABOARD!
ATTAGIRL!
NOW THAT THE MONSTERS, BOTH OLD AND NEW, WERE A MANAGEABLE SIZE, HOLLY WAS ABLE TO FOCUS ON HER JOURNEY.
LAND HO!
YOU WON'T LIKE IT WHEN YOU GET THERE!
THANKS, MIND!

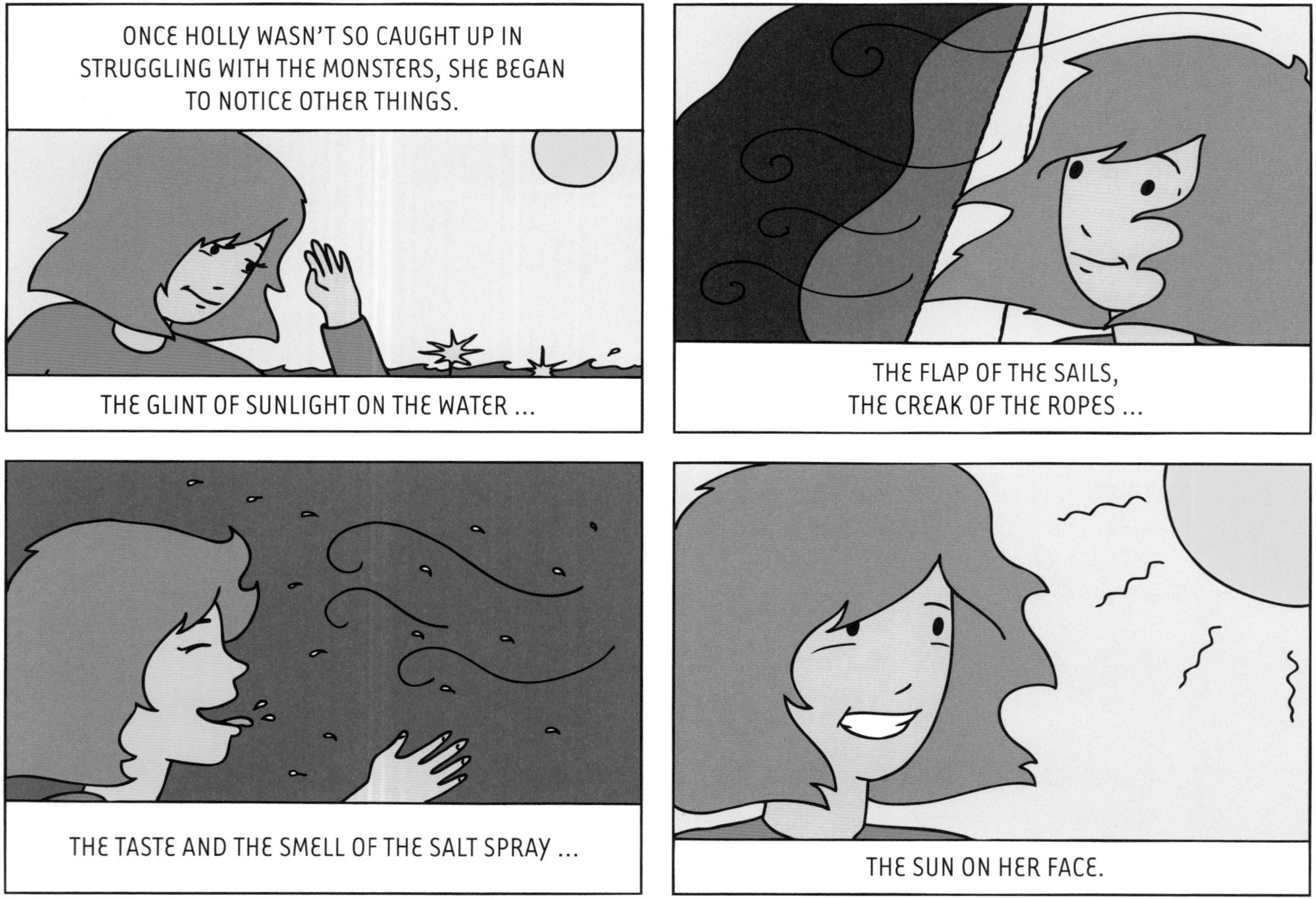
ONCE HOLLY WASN'T SO CAUGHT UP IN STRUGGLING WITH THE MONSTERS, SHE BEGAN TO NOTICE OTHER THINGS.
THE GLINT OF SUNLIGHT ON THE WATER ...
THE FLAP OF THE SAILS, THE CREAK OF THE ROPES ...
THE TASTE AND THE SMELL OF THE SALT SPRAY ...
THE SUN ON HER FACE.

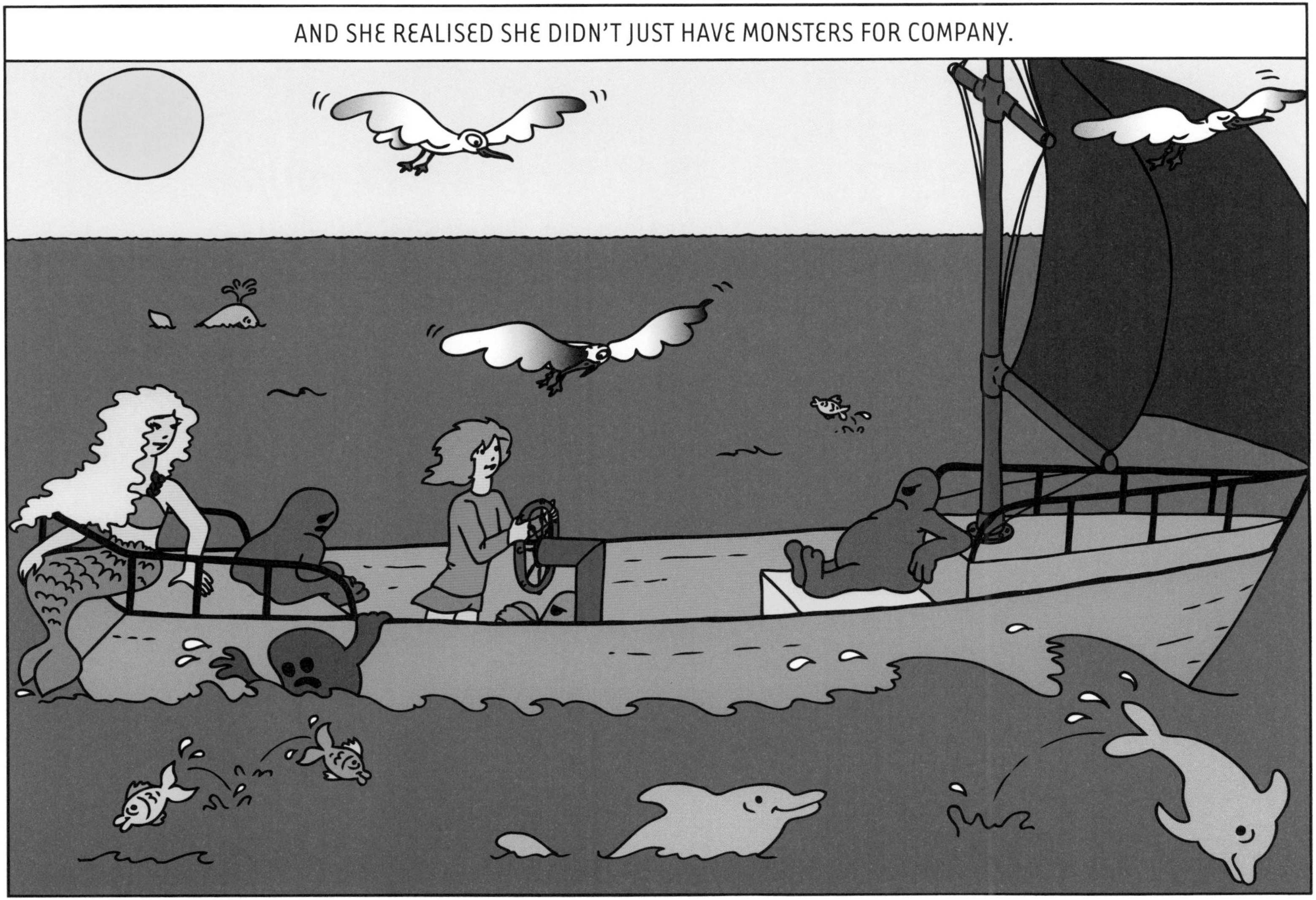
AND SHE REALISED SHE DIDN'T JUST HAVE MONSTERS FOR COMPANY.

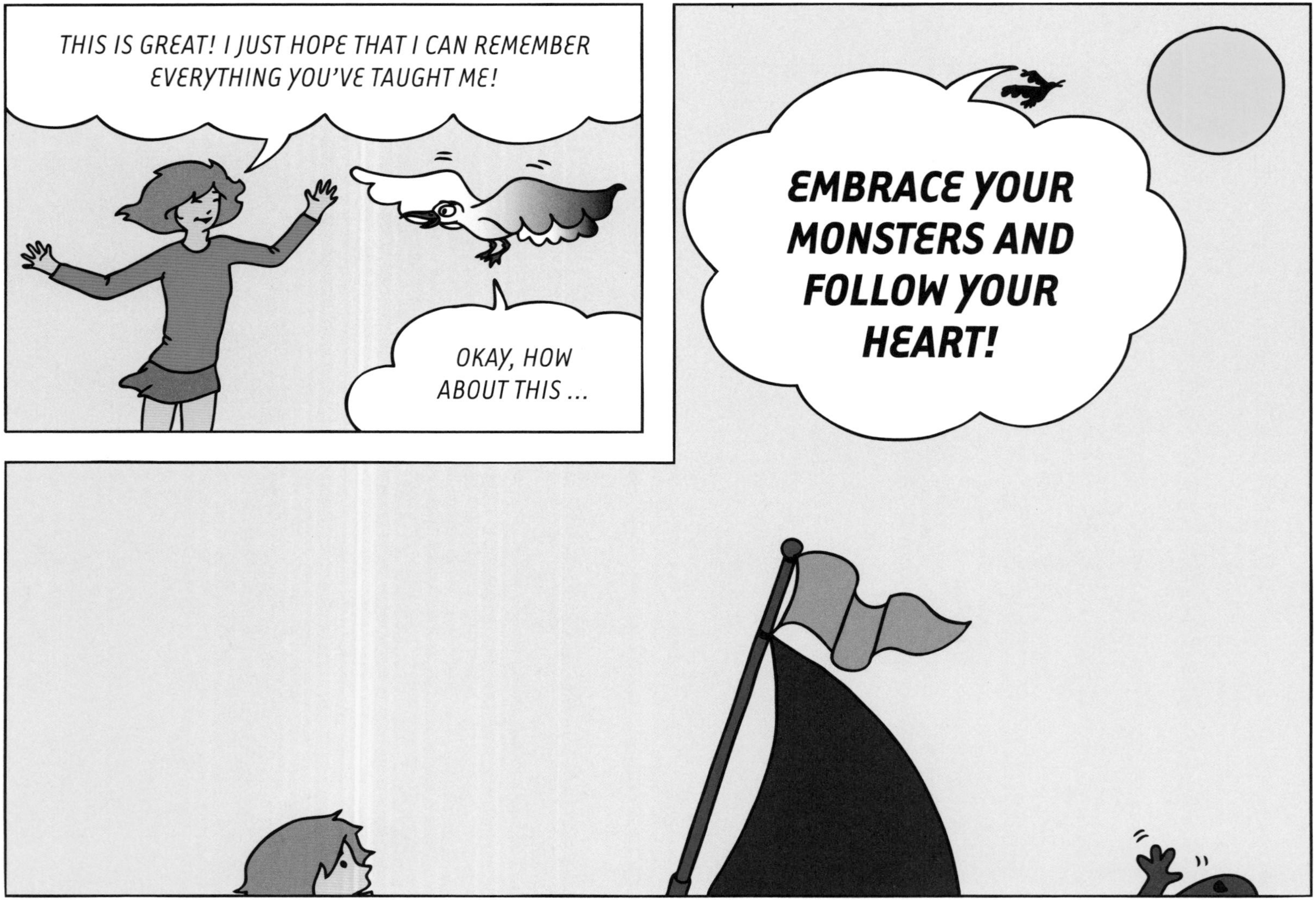
THIS IS GREAT! I JUST HOPE THAT I CAN REMEMBER EVERYTHING YOU'VE TAUGHT ME!
OKAY, HOW ABOUT THIS ...
EMBRACE YOUR MONSTERS AND FOLLOW YOUR HEART!

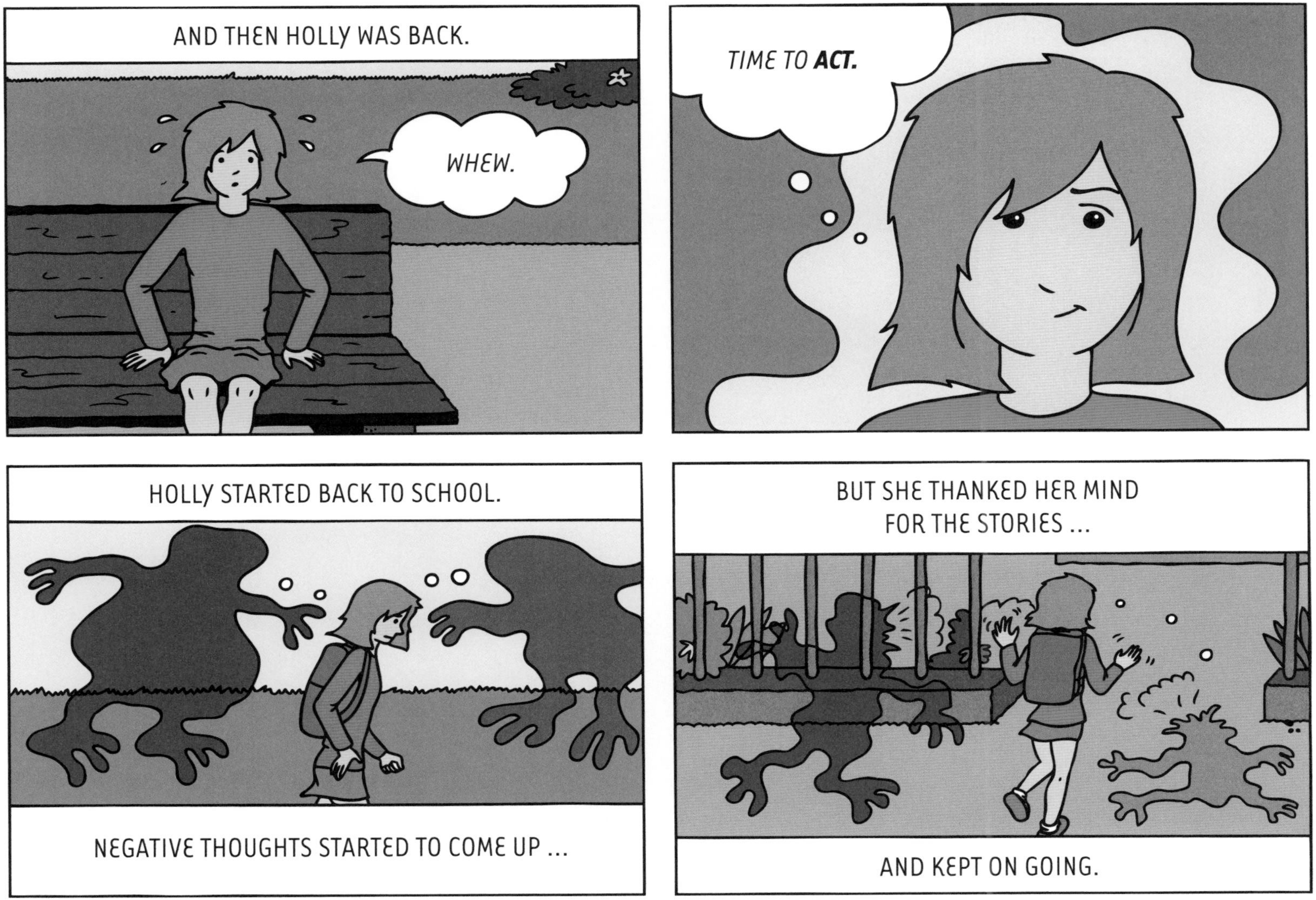
AND THEN HOLLY WAS BACK.
WHEW.
TIME TO ACT.
HOLLY STARTED BACK TO SCHOOL.
NEGATIVE THOUGHTS STARTED TO COME UP ...
BUT SHE THANKED HER MIND FOR THE STORIES ...
AND KEPT ON GOING.

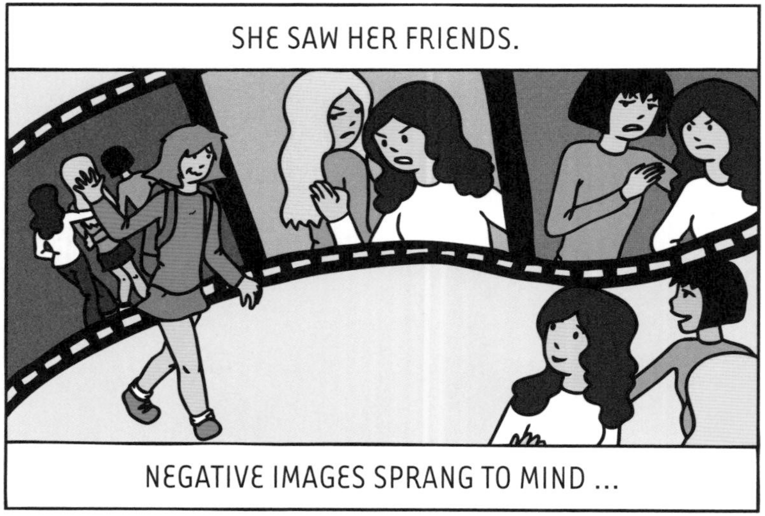
SHE SAW HER FRIENDS.
NEGATIVE IMAGES SPRANG TO MIND ...

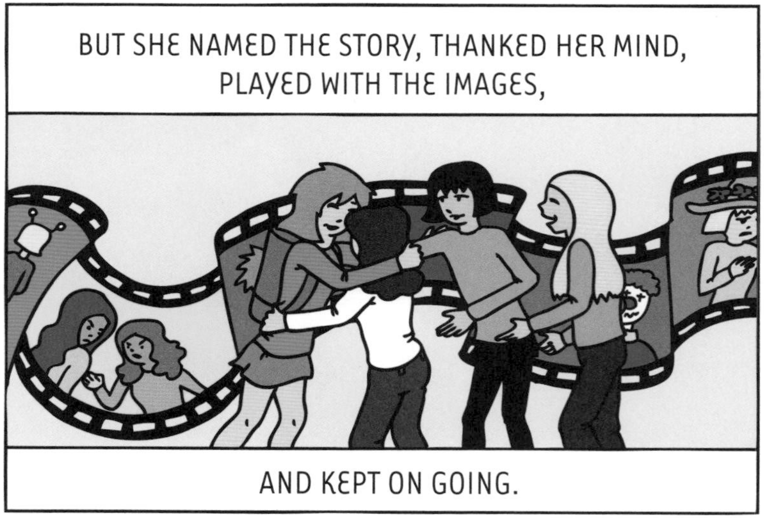
BUT SHE NAMED THE STORY, THANKED HER MIND, PLAYED WITH THE IMAGES,
AND KEPT ON GOING.

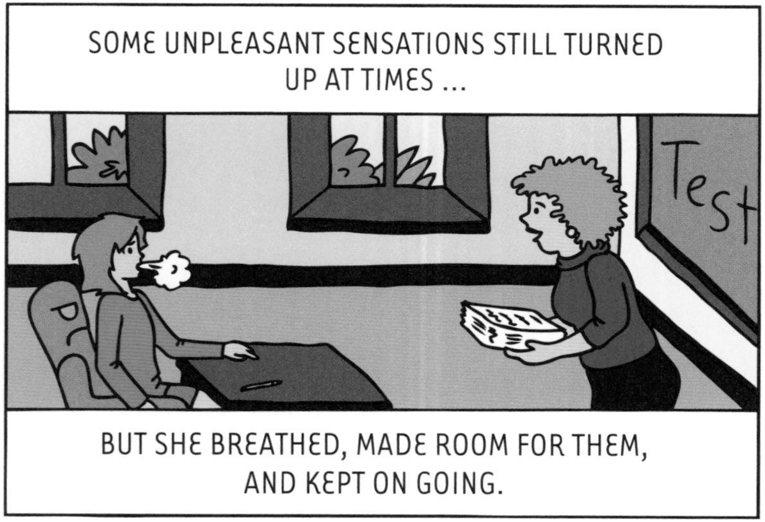
SOME UNPLEASANT SENSATIONS STILL TURNED UP AT TIMES ...
Test
BUT SHE BREATHED, MADE ROOM FOR THEM, AND KEPT ON GOING.

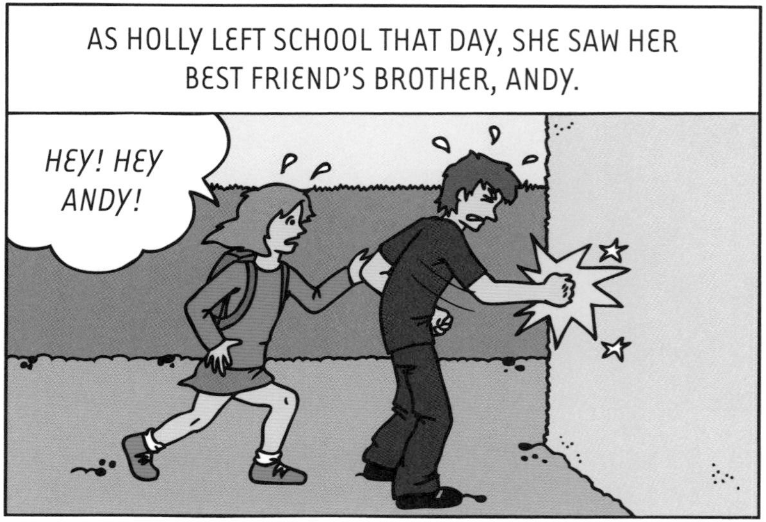
AS HOLLY LEFT SCHOOL THAT DAY, SHE SAW HER BEST FRIEND'S BROTHER, ANDY.
HEY! HEY ANDY!

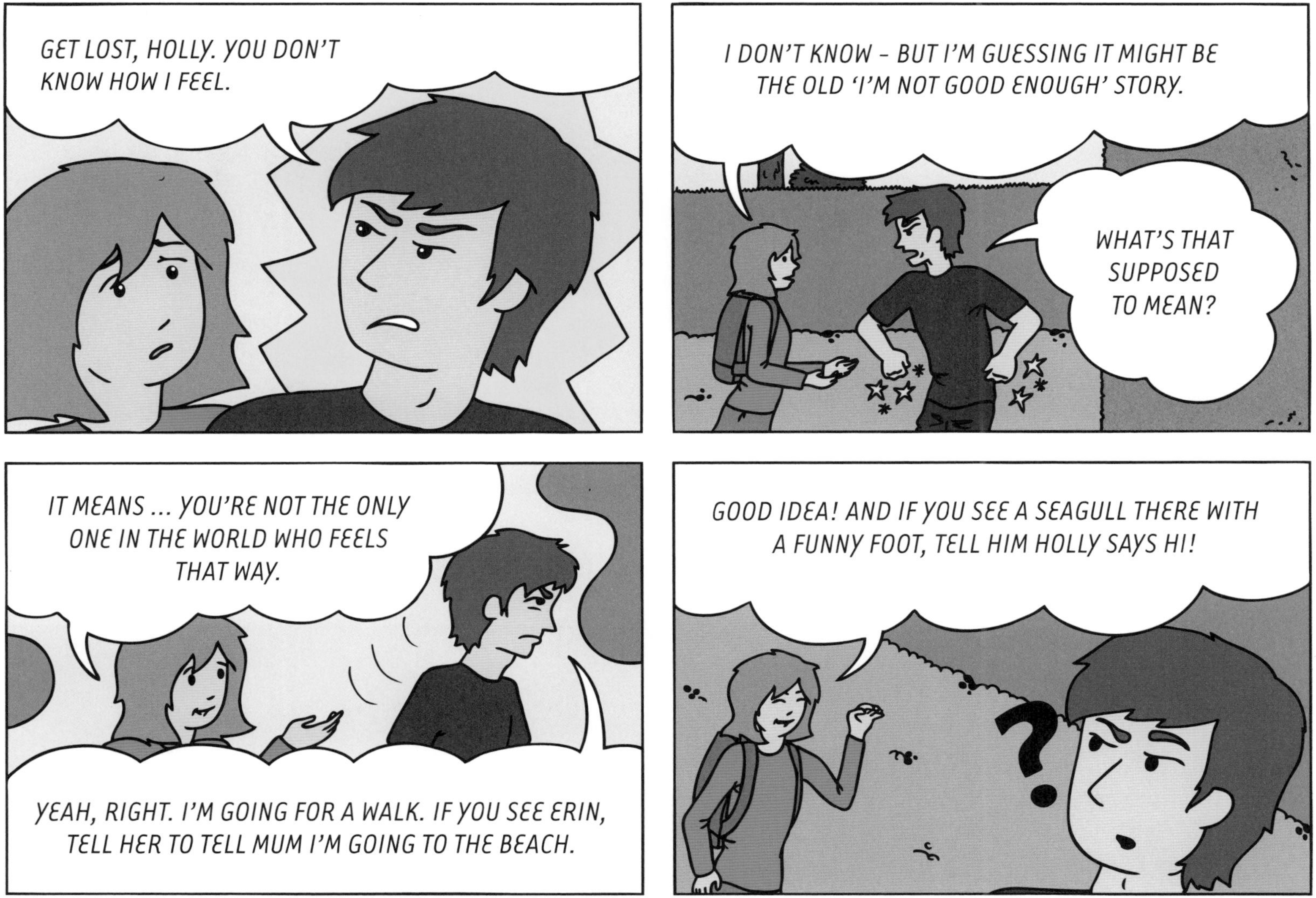
GET LOST, HOLLY. YOU DON'T KNOW HOW I FEEL.
I DON'T KNOW – BUT I'M GUESSING IT MIGHT BE THE OLD 'I'M NOT GOOD ENOUGH' STORY.
WHAT'S THAT SUPPOSED TO MEAN?
IT MEANS ... YOU'RE NOT THE ONLY ONE IN THE WORLD WHO FEELS THAT WAY.
YEAH, RIGHT. I'M GOING FOR A WALK. IF YOU SEE ERIN, TELL HER TO TELL MUM I'M GOING TO THE BEACH.
GOOD IDEA! AND IF YOU SEE A SEAGULL THERE WITH A FUNNY FOOT, TELL HIM HOLLY SAYS HI!
?

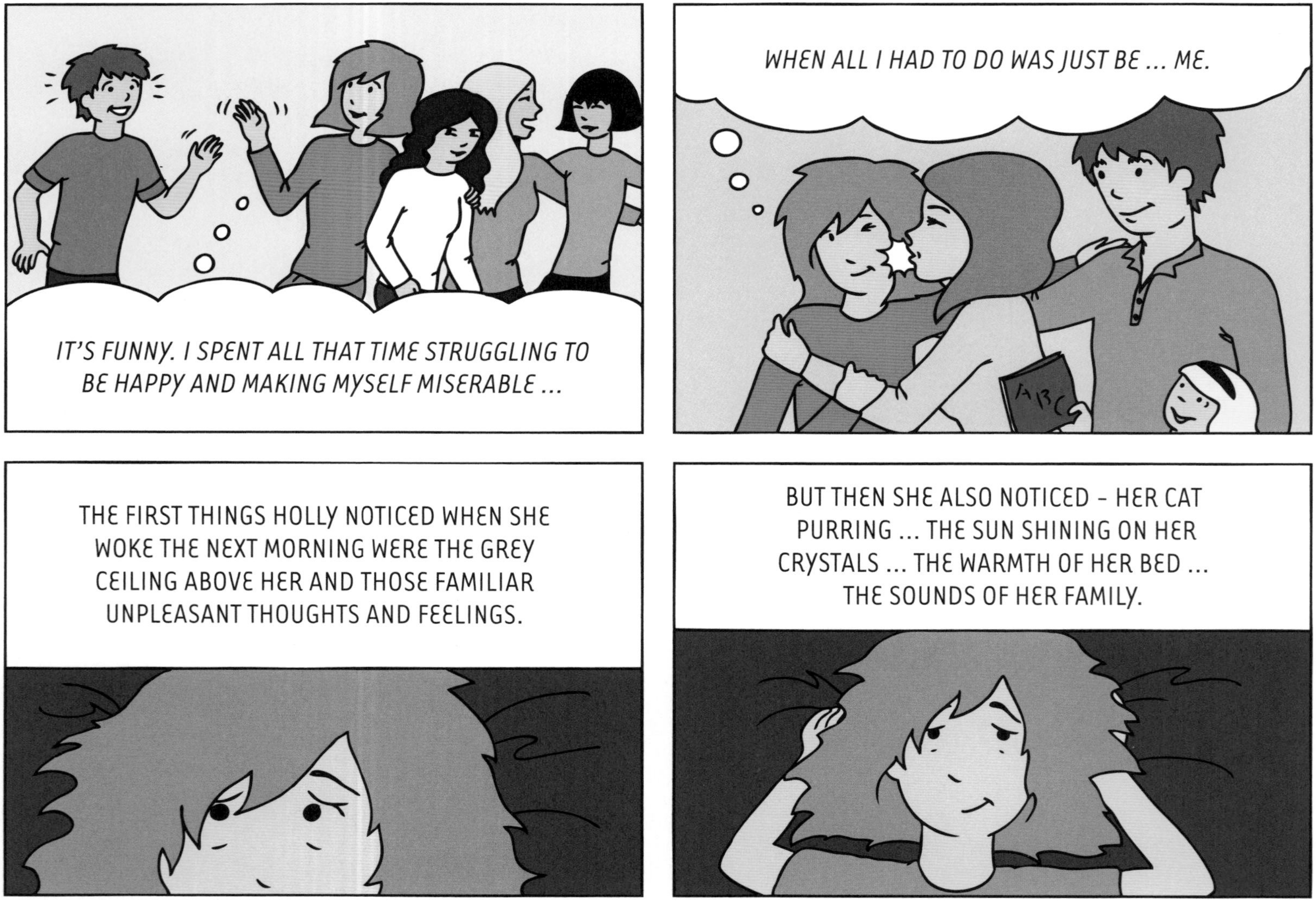
IT'S FUNNY. I SPENT ALL THAT TIME STRUGGLING TO BE HAPPY AND MAKING MYSELF MISERABLE ...
WHEN ALL I HAD TO DO WAS JUST BE ... ME.
THE FIRST THINGS HOLLY NOTICED WHEN SHE WOKE THE NEXT MORNING WERE THE GREY CEILING ABOVE HER AND THOSE FAMILIAR UNPLEASANT THOUGHTS AND FEELINGS.
BUT THEN SHE ALSO NOTICED – HER CAT PURRING ... THE SUN SHINING ON HER CRYSTALS ... THE WARMTH OF HER BED ... THE SOUNDS OF HER FAMILY.

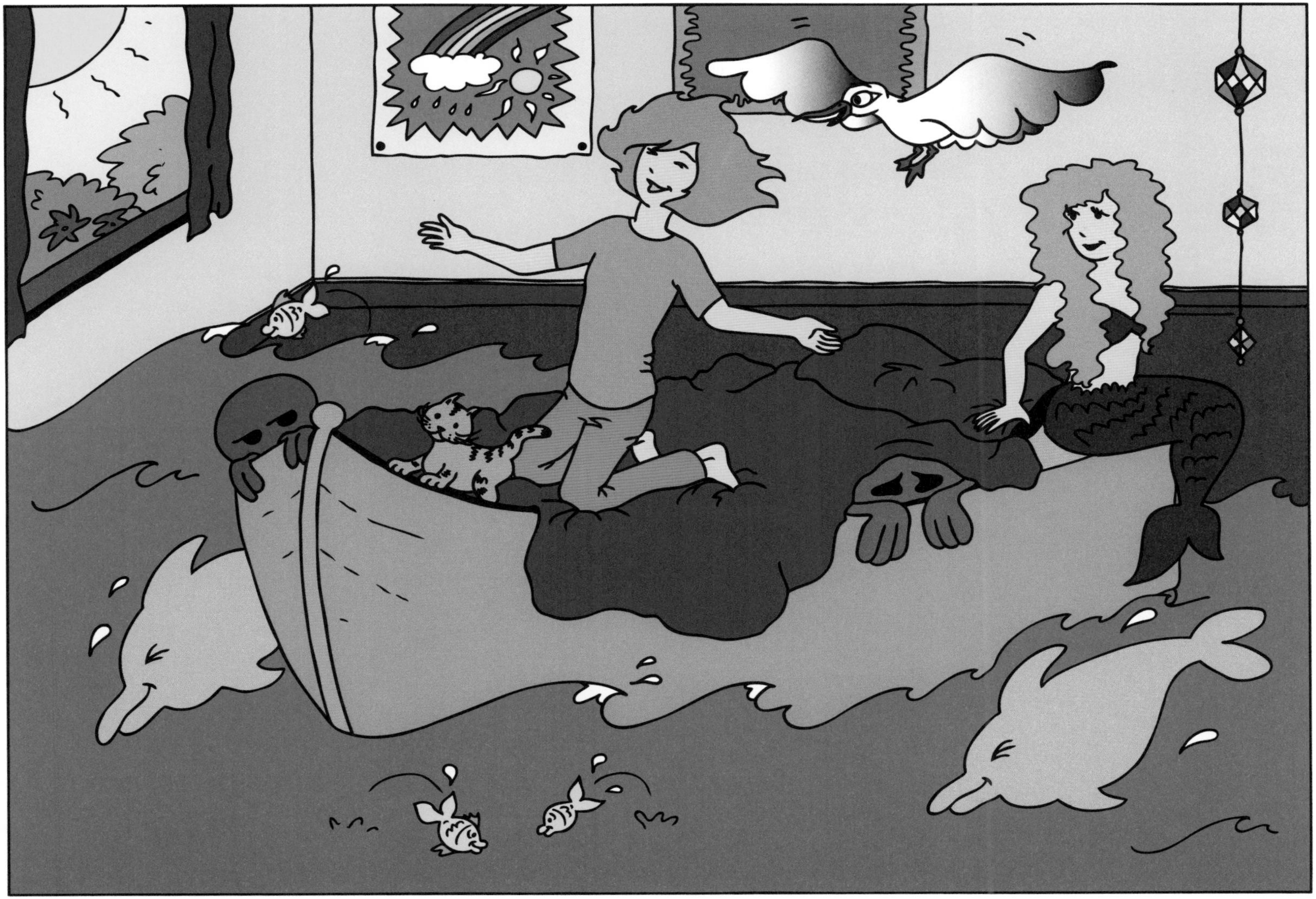

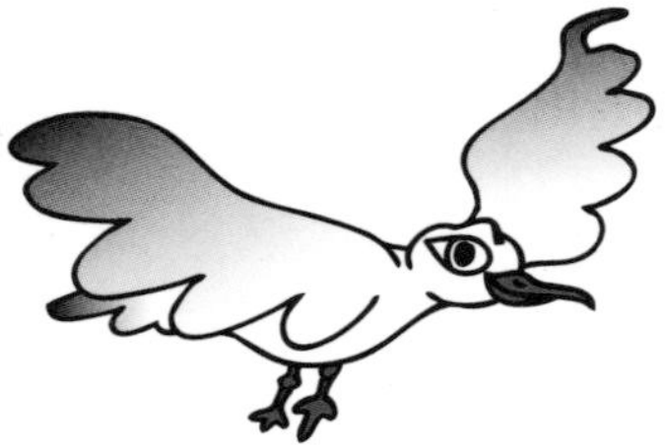

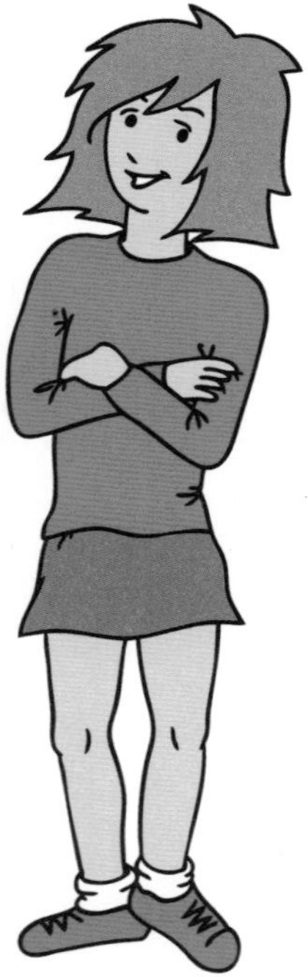

Acknowledgements

Firstly we would like to thank Dr Russ Harris for all his support — this book would not have been possible without him.

We also want to acknowledge the work of Steve Hayes, whose original 'passengers on a bus' ACT metaphor motivated Russ to go on and develop his own version, which in turn has led to our story.

The work of these two — and others at the forefront of the ACT community — has inspired and enriched our practice and our lives.

We hope this gives something back.

A big thank-you to the team at Exisle Publishing — Benny, Gareth, Al, Anouska and Tahnee. Their enthusiasm for the book and gentle handling of such publishing newbies has been greatly appreciated.

Resources

To download free resources for use with *I Just Want To Be ... ME!*, visit our website at **www.actonpurpose.com.au**. You can find a workbook for young people, guided discussion questions for parents and carers, and resources for classroom teachers and therapists.